AF264334

THE HAUNTED TRAIL

A Tale of Two Four-Leaf Clovers

By

John Lukegord

Copyright © 2024 John Lukegord

All rights reserved.

No portion of this book may be reproduced in any form without written permission from the publisher or author except as permitted by U.S. copyright law.

TABLE OF CONTENTS

CHAPTER 1

On a distant planet light-years away, two alien species were at war. These creatures had boundary lines to separate their territories. One of the species was green, and one was blue. The blue aliens had better technology than the green aliens. However, the green aliens possessed a rare artifact that the blue aliens were desperate to steal from them. This rare artifact was a four-leaf clover. On this mysterious alien planet, war towers defended each side of the boundary.

Exploding mines were a common weapon of defense for these aliens, but the blue aliens wore protective gear that was very durable. The green aliens' armor was made up of beryllium and would partially rupture and harm them if exposed to explosions. Both alien species had equipment to detect where these dangerous mines were located.

The aliens were genetically similar to humans. They required food and water to survive. Their planet had food-manufacturing facilities, water recycling plants, chemical engineering plants, power plants, medical treatment facilities, security facilities, and engineering schools for young aliens. There was also an oil refinery. These aliens couldn't speak, but both species were very creative and used sign language and sophisticated drawing to communicate. Regarding climate, the planet experienced wind, snow, and rain, as well as tornadoes, earthquakes, and hurricanes on occasion, but the advanced structural engineering of their buildings helped them withstand these natural disasters.

The green aliens kept a heavy guard on their rare four-leaf clover. They had mines surrounding certain areas around this rare artifact. The clover was kept in a chamber constructed of a scarce, indestructible alloy, which was found on their side of the planet. On the other side of the planet, where the blue aliens resided, this alloy was not scarce and was commonly used in their body suits, defense towers, and the construction of their spacecraft. There, blue aliens outnumbered the green species nearly twofold. There were 1,904 aliens on the planet; 1,208 of these aliens were blue, and the rest were green.

The alloy chamber in which the green aliens' clover resided was also a gravity device. The energy from the magical clover inside this protective mechanism allowed the four-leaf clover to float and spin inside it. The alloy protecting the clover did have a design flaw on the door. It was constructed of beryllium, which could be drilled through completely without damaging the other alloy in the protective chamber. It was designed this way to allow emergency access. The clover needed to be sprayed with purified water from their water treatment facility once a week, and the metal door was properly replaced each time the clover became hydrated.

The clover was also guarded by an electromagnetic current that was capable of immobilizing intruding blue aliens in their protective suits. The magnets were constructed 99 years ago, and they protected the area surrounding the clover, keeping it safe from theft. The electromagnets had stopped one invading blue alien in the past. The alien tried to steal the clover and got trapped in the electromagnets. The green aliens dismantled the blue alien's body armor and kept it, and the blue alien was executed for trespassing. The blue aliens now knew not to get too close to the electromagnets near the clover, as they didn't want their infantry getting stuck in them. They didn't want the green alien race getting their hands on any more of their technology.

The clover was found on this planet 100 years ago, at the bottom of a lake in a cave. Two genetically deformed aliens were born on Halloween night, a foot tall at birth. One of these aliens was a blue alien, and the other was a green alien; they were twins. They were both male. The green alien was born with a little blond beard. The blue alien was born with a black beard and a mustache. The strange thing about this blue creature was that it had a black birthmark on its chest, near its heart, that looked like a four-leaf clover.

A blue alien scientist had kidnapped and raped a female alien of the green species. The female alien was kept in a secured facility, and the green alien species went looking for her. The green female alien was given medicine and impregnated. The genetic result was that both of these aliens looked like little leprechauns, and they were hostile toward each other at birth. As a result, the blue alien scientist separated the mysterious creatures.

The blue aliens had just invented a technology that gave them protective body armor that was believed to be made out of indestructible material. They felt it was necessary for their own protection to wear this protective body armor while they conducted further studies on these two anomalies.

Through their scientific studies of these creatures, they discovered the twins were both born with unusual gifts. The small blue creature was very hostile and immune to sedatives. It had viciously sharp teeth and growled constantly. The strange gift this blue creature had was that it could chew through the alloy on the supposedly indestructible body armor the blue alien scientists had been wearing. It was fascinating, but they couldn't understand why. Test after test, this metal showed extreme durability to impact and heat. The scientists pondered this unique creature while five scientists desperately pried it off and calmed it down. Eventually, the blue alien did settle after the tests, and the restraints on it finally stopped.

The thing that made the little green leprechaun alien unique was that it could float. Gravity stabilizers had to be constructed all over the planet to stabilize it. This was another mysterious phenomenon because, according to the aliens' theories and the laws of physics, this was impossible.

The scientists thought the green alien's gift was just as interesting as the little blue alien's ability to chew through an indestructible alloy. They thought it was much too dangerous to operate on these creatures because of their abilities. The little green creature, much like its blue twin, was immune to sedatives.

The blue alien race held the green female alien against her will for years, studying her. The results on the green alien were inconclusive, as the scientists found no genetic similarities to why she gave birth to unique twins. Eventually, the green alien died of blood loss while undergoing scientific study, when the procedures got more complex. The scientists decided setting the creatures free and letting nature take its course was the best option. They would see if both these potentially dangerous individuals would reproduce, so they released them together into a lake.

The little green alien fled to its side of the lake. The blue alien gave chase but couldn't swim after its twin. Because the little green creature could defy the rules of gravity and float, it was a much more efficient and dynamic swimmer than the dangerous blue creature. The blue creature eventually fled to its side of the lake. Under the cave at the bottom of the lake was a secret entryway to both sides of the planet. There is an entryway on both sides. Each alien spotted the passageway on their side simultaneously and entered.

Beneath the cave under the lake were passages that led to hidden places on the planet. These creatures could both detect something supernatural beneath the core of their planet. Another small lake was the grounding point marking the end of both passageways. Three hundred feet below this planet was the lowest point where water exists. At the bottom, there was a magical, shiny, four-leaf clover. Both creatures were on the hunt for it.

They slipped down separate tunnels near each other and fell into the lake at the same time. The little green alien, being a much better swimmer, swam to the bottom of the lake a few seconds quicker than the blue creature hunting it. The green alien grabbed the clover and snagged it first. It had to cautiously hold this fragile clover without crushing it and swim away from the little blue alien, but the blue alien took a vicious bite of the green alien's face.

The green alien was blinded as it desperately fought off its evil twin. The blue alien attempted a second attack but failed as the little green creature desperately swam away faster than it ever had before, carefully holding the clover in its left palm. The green alien managed to swim above water, and then float upward with its gravity-defying ability. It latched onto the cave portal and escaped from the hostile little blue alien.

The blue alien experienced a sense of failure because it couldn't stop its enemy from fleeing with the clover. The angry, little blue alien had to slowly crawl up the rocks near the cave to get to the entryway back to its side of the planet. It fell a couple of times and couldn't figure out the proper coordination to climb back up the entryway to its side of the planet. Eventually, it learned more efficient climbing techniques and got to the high passageway, escaping from the cave.

It was reported back to the medical facility. It drew a picture in front of the blue alien scientist that had conducted experiments on it earlier that night, a picture of a shining four-leaf clover as well as a picture of its green twin. It pointed to both pictures with anger. The blue alien scientist was astonished. The little blue alien showed the scientist the entryway to the cave it had discovered. The scientists now had the knowledge that they could illegally sneak into the cave and thus gain access to the green aliens' side. The scientists began studying the terrain below the planet.

The little blue alien died shortly after revealing the hidden passageway to its scientist. It died from poisoning caused by chewing the alloy on the scientists' suits. The blue aliens constructed an oil refinery plant near the lake and conducted underground drilling beneath the planet. One of the purposes of this was to tap into oil wells at the core of the planet. The other was to study their enemies' side and plan a clover heist.

The green leprechaun had returned to its side of the planet, using its other senses because it was blind. When it made it back to a safe passage near the lake, it gave the clover to a green alien responsible for security near the lake. The alien security officer was amazed by this clover but also noticed that the little green alien was in trouble, as it was squealing. It died of blood loss right in front of the security guard. The bite from the little blue alien had slowly killed it.

The mysterious green little creature was buried respectfully in a grave, and the clover was kept and studied by the green aliens. The green aliens never found the female alien who had been kidnapped from their side of the planet, and they never found out how to access the two secret caves separating the planet, where this magical clover was found.

These events started the dangerous clover war on this mysterious alien planet. The green aliens had security cameras and mini-fighter jets surrounding the electromagnets that created the force field around the magical clover. The clover had been under security by the green aliens for 100 years. For all those years, the blue aliens had planned to steal this magical clover from the green aliens.

After a century of secret drilling, the blue aliens executed their attack on Halloween night and launched bombs beneath the ground under the clover device. The ground collapsed, and the clover device fell fifty feet into the planet. The clover device remained intact after it had fallen. The green aliens couldn't survive the bomb blast because their battle suits caught fire. Most of them died instantly from burns when their battle suits failed them.

The green aliens activated the electromagnets, but many of their own got trapped in them. The blue aliens could now approach the clover chamber without being affected by the magnets. The blue aliens took mini lasers to the metal door and accessed the rare clover. The blue alien race stole the four-leaf clover and quickly escaped from the area, setting off more bombs behind them.

They headed through passageways they had constructed below the planet. Four blue aliens entered a spaceship and fled the planet with the clover. The green aliens immediately began devising a strategy to get the clover back. Four green aliens left the planet in two small spacecraft, with two aliens aboard each. One of the green aliens wore the battle suit that their race had stolen from the blue aliens almost a century ago.

An all-out war broke out. In retaliation for the clover theft, the green aliens detonated a bomb on the blue aliens' soil, right next to a nuclear power plant. When the bomb exploded, the air surrounding the mysterious planet became contaminated with plutonium, uranium, and other hazardous chemicals. The air became highly toxic. Both alien species had protective breathing masks connected to their battle suits, but the breathing masks only kept both alien species alive for a few days after the nuclear explosion.

Within a week, food and water supplies became contaminated, and all the aliens died of radiation poisoning. The planet became uninhabitable. Then, the core of the planet became unstable. The planet eventually exploded. Both alien species nearly became extinct.

CHAPTER 2

In Dublin, Ireland, an impoverished family was desperate to hold on to every moment they had with a dying family member. Harvard McPherson was dying of an unknown disease. Harvard had a wife named Betty and a six-year-old son named Butch. Harvard was the manager and part-owner of a local bakery in Dublin. Betty had never trusted her husband's business partner, a disgruntled baker named Curtis Haynesworth.

Harvard McPherson and Curtis Haynesworth had been really good friends until a dispute got in the way and ultimately ruined their friendship. Before Harvard got sick, they had become business partners. They ran a bakery together downtown called the Dublin Express Bakery. They were successful. A few years into the bakery's success, however, Harvard started showing up to work really sick. He was weak in the bones and, sometimes, he struggled to breathe and talk.

He would cough all the time and, over the course of a few days, the strange illness became much worse. Harvard showed up to work that day at 10:20 a.m. He was supposed to show up at 7:00 a.m.

"Where the fuck have you been, man?" said Curtis. "You're over three hours late, for Christ's sake."

"I'm sorry about that," said Harvard. "My wife was out fishing on the Dublin River this morning. She was trying to catch some fish so we can put some new shit on our menu for a change. Our son wasn't feeling well today, so he stayed home from school, and I had to stay home with him and watch him while she was out."

"Did she even catch any fish this morning?" asked Curtis.

"No, she didn't," said Harvard. "She was out there for a few hours and didn't catch anything. It was a shit day of fishing out there on the river for her today. Sorry about that, man."

"First of all," said Curtis, "you being here on time to run this fuckin' place is more important than your family business. Second, she didn't catch shit out there today, so it sounds like it was a total waste of fuckin' time. You've been very flakey lately, and it seems like, for the past few days, there's always something holding you back from showing up on time. Get your shit together and show the fuck up on time and help me run this goddamn fuckin' place! I can't do it with just this little shit Todd helping me out in the morning. He's incapable of doing certain tasks efficiently. Plus, he has to go to school at noon today."

Harvard lowered his head. "Again, I apologize about this. I'll try to be here on time from now on."

"You better get your ass here on time from now on because I can't run this fuckin' place with just this little shithead kid," said Curtis.

"Alright, man. You're repeating yourself. I read you loud and clear. I'll show up on time from now on," said Harvard.

"Ok," said Curtis. "That sounds good. Let's forget about this bullshit and get to work."

They both went back to work after the conversation ended. An hour passed. Harvard was about to take a customer's order when he suddenly became very dizzy.

"Hello, Sir, welcome to the...welcome to the...welcome to the Dublin, to the Dublin, to the Dublin Express," Harvard stuttered.

The customer looked at Harvard oddly because something about Harvard's mannerisms seemed off. Then, a few seconds later, Harvard collapsed to the floor. Everyone in the bakery who had witnessed this was shocked and became worried about Harvard. A nervous 13-year-old employee named Todd Flanagan ran over to Harvard and tried to help revive him.

"Mr. McPherson, are you alright?" asked Todd.

Harvard didn't respond because he wasn't coherent. When Todd was a few feet away from Harvard, Curtis stepped in, grabbed Todd tightly by the back of the neck, and shoved him a few feet out of the way.

"Mind your damn business, kid, and get back to work!" said Curtis to the timid employee.

Todd put his head down in shame, rubbed the back of his neck, and went back to cleaning tables. Curtis took a stand and did what he thought was best for the business. "Everyone, please try to stay calm and give me a few minutes to sort out the chaos!"

The crowd of customers began talking among each other with curiosity.

"Harvard! Harvard! Can you hear me? Snap out of it and try to open your eyes, buddy!" said Curtis as he lightly shook Harvard.

Harvard was at first unresponsive. Then, about a minute later, Harvard opened his eyes. "What the fuck just happened?" he asked.

"You passed out a few minutes ago," said Curtis.

"Man, I feel like dog shit," said Harvard.

"I'm going to drag you into the inventory room. Just lay there and try to relax," said Curtis. Harvard rested on the floor while his partner slowly dragged him across the back kitchen of the bakery and into the inventory room. Curtis said to Harvard, "Jesus, man! You're really fuckin' sick. Do you know what's wrong with you?"

Harvard replied, "No. All I know is that this morning before work, Dr. Kellis told me I have an incurable illness. I had a seven o'clock appointment with Dr. Kellis this morning. That's why I showed up to work three hours late today. I'm a little embarrassed about this sickness. I should have just been honest with you earlier this morning about why I was late instead of making up some bullshit excuse that my son needed someone to look after him when Betty was actually home to take care of him. My son went to school this morning, and he wasn't even sick. Unfortunately, I'm the one who's sick. That whole story about her fishing on the Dublin River was nothing but a big fuckin' lie. I just didn't want to admit I was ill because it's been so rough on me and the family.

"I'm sorry I've been covering up the fact I have health problems. I felt fine a few weeks ago. Then, all of a sudden, this mysterious disease came about. I have no fuckin' clue how I became sick, and I can barely afford to go to any more doctor appointments. I just feel like resting in a fuckin' hospital bed for the rest of my worthless life. This is a very difficult disease to battle, and I'm doing the best I can to keep a good attitude. I need to take care of my family with the rest of the money I have for the week. I don't have a lot of cash on hand because everything is invested in our bakery. Oh, this fuckin' blows donkey dick!" shouted Harvard in misery as he was lying there on the dirty kitchen floor in the inventory room shaken up.

"Look, Harvard, you have my deepest sympathy. However, you're way too goddamn sick to run this fuckin' place anymore. You need to do what's best for your health, man. You should step down permanently. I'll buy you out and run the bakery from now on."

"I think you're right. My sickness is beginning to ruin the integrity of this little hole-in-the-wall bakery. I should just take a giant step back from all this bakery shit and be with my family. I like the idea of you buying me out. How much is this fuckin' shithole worth, anyway?"

"One thousand dollars."

"I thought it would be worth closer to two thousand with our success this year."

"Inventory, maintenance, and hired labor have taken a heavy toll on our profits."

"Well, then why the fuck did you hire that Flanagan kid last week if things have been tight lately?"

"I hired him because you haven't been around here quite as much over the last few weeks, and we were desperate for extra help. I know the kid is a little pussy, but I'll keep him around for a few more weeks until someone better suited for the job comes along."

"You should just spare the kid the trouble and get rid of his incompetent ass today."

"Believe me, man, I would if I could, but we're way too short-staffed right now."

The conversation ended. Curtis went back to work, and Harvard stayed in the inventory room and rested. The staff at the Dublin Express Bakery did the best they could to run the place despite what had happened.

However, Curtis was conning his sick partner. He was in charge of the books and accounting for the bakery. He'd been secretly embezzling from the company and taking much more than his agreed-upon cut of the profits. Harvard was unaware of this because he was responsible for the baking. He was the head baker of the business.

The buyout his partner was offering did seem a little bit less than Harvard expected, but he still took the offered amount. Curtis Haynesworth gave his partner $500 for his cut of the bakery business. The buyout felt a little short to Harvard, and he was reluctant to take the $500 buyout on impulse. Harvard hadn't looked at the company books in the last ten months. Harvard was unaware of the true worth of this bakery because he'd partnered up with a scam artist. Harvard was also becoming delusional and not all there, mentally. Haynesworth could see this, so he exploited his sick friend and took unfair advantage of him. Their bakery business was really worth closer to two grand. The chaotic day at the Dublin Express Bakery came to an end at 9:00 p.m. when Haynesworth closed the doors.

***

The next day, just before heading to the bakery, Curtis went to the private office of a doctor he knew named Thadius Roberts to speak with him about Harvard's illness. Curtis knocked at the front door of the house and a minute later Thadius opened the door.

"Curtis, what the hell are you doing here?" Thadius said. "This better be damn important. You know that I like to keep a low profile in this town because my reputation as a doctor is practically ruined."

"I know you like to keep a low profile around here, and I'm sorry for just randomly showing up at your front door like this," replied Curtis. "But trust me, this is damn important."

"Then what the fuck is this about?" asked Thadius.

"It's about my business partner, Harvard McPherson," said Curtis. "He is very ill right now. He has some kind of strange illness, and he desperately needs some treatment. His current doctor sounds like he is very incompetent and can't do shit for him. I suspect that my business partner has been skimming from the profits over the last couple of weeks so that he can pay for his treatment. I just bought him out for his cut of the business for $500 yesterday. I should have given him double the amount of money that I gave him. I already fucked him over, but I want to get back at him again because of this betrayal."

"It sounds like your partner is in a world of shit right now," said Thadius. "Ok, I've got an idea. Tell the man that I have recently created a new vaccine and that I need $500 to treat his illness. If you can convince him that this medicine is the real deal, we will fuck him over and then split the money fifty-fifty."

"Ok, I will do so," Curtis said. "That sounds perfect. Harvard has the money to cover the treatment plan if he decides to go forward with it. I'll do my best to persuade him. Hopefully, the asshole believes what I'm telling him and I can fuck him over twice. I'm heading over to his house right now to speak with him."

Thadius nodded. "Ok. You have my permission to bring the man to my house for the treatment. I'll be waiting to hear back from you."

"Take care, Thadius."

After his conversation with the doctor, Curtis paid his ill friend Harvard a visit to his house. The front door was unlocked. Curtis opened up the front door and walked into the house. Curtis said to Harvard, "Your front door was unlocked, so I let myself in."

"That's fine. What's up, man?" said Harvard as he lay on his couch in agony.

Curtis said to Harvard, "You know, I feel terrible about your illness. I know a brilliant doctor who can help you. I went to his private office this morning and spoke to him about your strange illness. He told me he has created a new vaccine and that he needs $500 to treat you with the vaccine for your illness."

Harvard coughed a few times and replied, "Who the fuck is he, and what can he do about my sickness?"

"His name is Thadius Roberts. He's the best doctor in Ireland. I know what Dr. Kellis said to you about this mysterious disease being incurable. Dr. Roberts might be able to help keep you alive for this kind of money. I know it's every damn cent I gave you for the bakery business, but I'm telling you, as a friend, that this guy, Dr. Roberts, can help prolong your life. He knows a whole lot more about medicine than that fuckin' idiot, Dr. Kellis. He was denied the right to legally perform surgeries as a doctor on any living person after he tried to put wings on a human being in a science lab to see if his test subject could fly. The experiment was shut down by other scientists frustrated by his dangerous experiment.

That's the only reason he isn't a licensed doctor anymore. He likes to keep a very low profile as a doctor in this town after his ruined reputation. He is hated by many other doctors because of these experiments, but I'm telling you the fuckin' guy is brilliant. I know him personally, and I go to his private office whenever I need medical treatment. Don't let his shady reputation fool you. He's a brilliant doctor, and I can introduce you to him if you'd like."

"Yes, for the love of god, please. Set up the fuckin' appointment as soon as possible."

Betty was in the kitchen cutting potatoes and had only heard bits and pieces of the conversation between Curtis and her husband. Betty didn't care to go into the other room to say hello to him. Curtis only stayed at their house for five minutes, then he left and headed to work.

As soon as Haynesworth left, Betty went into the other room to speak to her husband. "You know," she said, "I think that Haynesworth is full of shit. Whoever the hell this Dr. Roberts is, there's a legitimate reason why he isn't allowed to legally operate on patients anymore. I think you should keep going to Dr. Kellis instead. He only charges you five cents per visit. This Dr. Roberts guy wants $500 to treat your disease. That's absurd. Dr. Kellis has confirmed there's no cure or official diagnosis for your mysterious illness. This 'Dr. Roberts' idea that that asshole baker Haynesworth has you so convinced of sounds like a big medical scam."

"Dr. Kellis isn't doing anything to make me feel any better," said Harvard, between coughs. "I'm going to try this Dr. Roberts instead. He sounds like a smart guy."

"I think you're being tricked by your best friend. I think you should give me the $500 right now because you're delusional, and you seem very tempted to spend it all on this sketchy experimental treatment. This guy Roberts sounds like a shady doctor."

"I'm sorry, honey, but I've made up my mind," Harvard said. "I might be delusional, but I'm not a fuckin' idiot. I'm not giving you my damn money. I'm desperate right now, so I'll take my chances with Dr. Roberts. I trust in Haynesworth's word. We worked side by side at this crappy little bakery since we were twelve years old, both busting our asses. Then, three years ago, we finally became co-owners of the Dublin Express. We both got thirty years of labor invested into this fuckin' shithole. Haynesworth is my best friend, and he'd never fuck me over." Harvard coughed loudly.

"Don't waste all of the damn bakery money on this bullshit medicine scam. This is nonsense, Harvard. I think you need a new best friend," said Betty. She stormed out of the living room.

Harvard just rested on the couch. He could barely hold a thought. But his stubborn mind was made up about undergoing this experimental medical procedure.

Curtis set the appointment up. A day later, he introduced his sick friend to Dr. Thadius Roberts. Curtis went to the bakery after the brief introduction.

Thadius said, "Hello, Harvard. It's a pleasure to meet you. I'm sorry to hear about this mysterious illness. I'm here to assist you with your health in any way I can."

"Thank you, Dr. Roberts. But what exactly is it you can do for me?"

"I have experimental medicine I can provide for you. I invented the medicine myself. It's only been tested on animals and one other person."

"Is it dangerous?"

"Not according to the tests I've conducted on dogs, squirrels, raccoons, and one volunteer human being."

"What the hell kind of medicine is this exactly?"

"It's a powerful sedative that will help you rest comfortably tonight, then give you energy the very next day. By the looks of your condition, you'll need two doses to help keep you alive for a few more weeks. I can give you the first injection of the sedative right after I receive payment from you, and then I can give you the second injection in a week. Unfortunately, that's the best I can do for you. Mr. McPherson, I'm very sorry, but you're going to die from this illness."

Tears poured from Mr. McPherson's eyes. "Jesus, I have a six-year-old son. I'm not ready to leave this poor fuckin' kid behind."

"Again, Mr. McPherson, I'm very sorry about this, but this is the best I can do for you."

Harvard put his head down in a deep depression. Dr. Roberts patted him on the back.

"I'll give you the room for a moment, Mr. McPherson," said Dr. Roberts.

"Thank you, Doctor."

Dr. Roberts left the room and gave Harvard a few moments to himself. Then he went back into the room, where he found Harvard resting on the medical bed with a worried look on his face. The doctor collected the $500 from Harvard and gave him the sedative by injecting it into his veins with a needle. The medicine was in truth a basic treatment for the common cold that doctors used to treat people suffering from immune deficiencies. The doctor had severely overcharged Mr. McPherson.

Harvard left the doctor's office and walked home. His left arm felt a little sore from the medicine injection, but the soreness was nothing compared to the pain that he felt from his illness. When Harvard walked into his house, Betty was in the living room doing some house chores. "Hi, honey. How are you feeling?" she asked.

"I feel like crap. I just got a very powerful sedative injected into my left arm, and I'm really fuckin' tired. I am supposed to get another injection of the sedative in a week if I even make it until then. I just want to rest on the couch. Please just leave me the fuck alone and give me the damn room to myself for a little while."

"I'm sorry to hear that you feel like shit. I hope you feel better soon."

"Thanks for the support, honey, but there is no such thing as hope anymore with this terrible fuckin' disease that I'm suffering from."

Betty left the room feeling miserable about her husband's health condition. She walked into her kitchen and began to cry quietly.

***

Later that night, toward 9:00 p.m., Curtis closed the doors to his bakery and headed to Dr. Roberts' office. He arrived there at 9:15 p.m. Curtis knocked on the door, and Dr. Roberts answered.

"Hello, Curtis," said Dr. Roberts.

"Hey. How are you?" asked Curtis.

"I'm well. And you?" asked Dr. Roberts.

"I'm alright now that the fuckin' bakery is closed for the night. So, how did the medicine scam go?" asked Curtis.

"It went perfectly as planned, my friend," said Dr. Roberts.

"Oh, so the stupid fuck fell for it," said Curtis.

"Yes, he did. Your former business partner looks like shit from his disease," Dr. Roberts said. "But as long as we got his $500, then who gives a flying fuck about his health? The man is going to die soon, and we sucked him dry for all of his coins."

"Yes, we did," said Curtis.

"Here is the $250 that I owe you," said Dr. Roberts, handing the cash to Curtis.

"Thanks for the cash," said Curtis. "It was a pleasure doing business with you."

"Same here, my friend. Take care."

"You as well."

The two men then shook hands. Then Curtis left the office and headed home.

***

The next day, Harvard didn't feel any better. He was so sick. The medicine had barely worked. A day later, he became very weak again. He didn't have any energy to get up. He couldn't walk, so he just rested on the couch in his living room.

Betty McPherson was very upset. She yelled out, "That cheap scoundrel Haynesworth fucked us over on the profits. The damn bakery is worth at least twice the amount of money that cheap asshole bought us out for. And, on top of that, that medicine scam you were tricked into paying all of our $500 bucks for from that screwball Dr. Roberts was a fuckin' joke. I could've made you some hot tea as a home remedy for free. You're on the verge of dying, and these people fucked us over. Haynesworth is supposed to be your friend? Well, fuck him!"

"Haynesworth and I used to have a partnership. He set me up with a brilliant doctor. The medicine barely did anything because I'm really fuckin' sick right now, and there's no cure for this godawful disease. I've only gotten one injection of the sedative from the fuckin' doctor so far! I'm supposed to get the second injection next week. I told you that a couple of days ago, right when I got home from the fuckin' doctor's office for Christ's sake! I just need to stay patient for a week, so get off my fuckin' case about this, you heartless bitch! I'm dealing with enough fuckin' stress as it is, and I'm really getting sick of hearing you badmouthing Haynesworth. He's my friend."

Harvard coughed, harshly.

"Your friend?" Betty laughed. "He's your friend? That selfish asshole took advantage of you. What kind of friend would do something like that? Huh? Every time I step foot into that fuckin' bakery, that slimy bastard gives me a perverted look. Let me tell you how off-putting that is. That goddamn bakery business turned Haynesworth into a greedy asshole. And you're so fuckin' delusional from this disease you can't even see your best friend fucked you over."

"OK. I get it. You don't like the fuckin' guy! Let's just stop talking about this. Our son is in the other room, and he doesn't need to hear this shit."

Butch, their six-year-old son, overheard his mother badmouthing Mr. Haynesworth. He couldn't just sit there and do nothing while his ill father suffered. On this Halloween night, Butch McPherson planned a cash heist at the Dublin Express to get his family the financial push they needed.

Butch knew Haynesworth would be at the annual Dublin Halloween Fair a few blocks over from the bakery shop. Haynesworth sold his bread at the fair to feed the locals and promote his business. Haynesworth kept $100 in a cash register. He also kept the key to his cash register on him at all times, but the register could potentially be pried open. The bakery was empty.

Butch walked up to his father and said, "I'm sorry about your strange illness, Pop. Thank you for working all those long days at the bakery for our family. It's my turn to pay you back."

Harvard coughed a few times, looked at his son oddly, and said, "What the fuck are you talking about, kid?" Harvard McPherson was dizzy. He could barely see or hear. But he heard what his son had said, and he had no idea why his six-year-old boy would say this to him. He underestimated his son's determination.

Harvard just lay there, suffering on the couch in his living room, extremely sick, shivering uncontrollably. He shut his eyes. He was becoming even weaker.

Butch didn't reply. He grabbed a crowbar from his father's toolshed and stormed out of the house, very pissed off. He was only six, but even he could see his father deserved a whole lot more for how hard the man had worked. Butch had often seen that asshole Mr. Haynesworth count handfuls of cash and stash it in his cash register with a greedy look on his face. He knew that much more of that cash belonged to his father.

Butch was dressed all in black. The bakery was a mile from his house, but there was a shortcut through the woods. The only thing going through Butch's mind as he trotted through the woods was what a fuckin' scumbag Haynesworth was and how badly he wanted to steal all his cash.

Butch was almost at the bakery. He walked down McWitham Street and looked around this small side street to see if it was clear. The street was empty; however, 328 people were a few blocks over at the Dublin Halloween Fair.

Curtis Haynesworth was at the Dublin Halloween Fair with his helper Todd Flanagan, selling milk, bread, biscuits, and tea. Haynesworth was low on biscuits. He had an emergency supply of a dozen biscuits he'd left behind at his bakery. He said, "Hey, Flanagan, I'm heading over to the bakery to get more biscuits. I'll be right back. I'm depending on you to take charge of the sales booth on your own for just a little while. Try not to fuck things up while I'm gone. Alright, kid?"

He rubbed the top of Todd's head, and Todd tensed up for a few seconds. Haynesworth left the sales booth and headed a few blocks over to his bakery.

Butch had just arrived at the bakery. He ran to the back. The back door was locked; there was a giant padlock on the back door.

Butch looked at a small window below the left side of the back door. He walked up to the little window, his crowbar in hand. Butch leaned over and began tugging the crowbar at the window, attempting to force it open. After successfully prying open the window, he cracked the little lock and the wooden frame around the window.

He wiggled himself inside the bakery. Butch knew where the cash register was. He ran over to it, his crowbar in hand. He jimmied the cash register door open in a few seconds. He looked inside and saw a wad of cash. There was $100 in the cash register. Butch grinned as he grabbed the money and pocketed it. He grabbed his crowbar and headed back to the little window. He hopped up to it and wiggled his small body through it.

Curtis Haynesworth had just arrived at his bakery. When he walked over to the back door, he looked over to his left and saw Butch McPherson crawling out of a window. He became enraged and yelled at Butch, "Hey, McPherson! What the hell are you doing in my bakery?"

Butch looked up. Then he got up and ran.

Haynesworth gave chase. "I'm going to get you, you little bastard!" he yelled as he chased up the hill after the boy. Butch kept running. He didn't look back. Butch ran up the hill as the angry baker followed, determined to catch him.

Butch reached the top of the hill and tripped on a bright green patch of grass. He looked down at the grass and saw a bright, shiny, four-leaf clover right in front of his eyes. He opened his eyes a little wider, then grabbed the little charm with his left hand and stashed it in the left pocket of his jacket.

Butch was tightly holding his crowbar in his right hand. Haynesworth was five feet away from him. Butch turned around and looked at Haynesworth.

Haynesworth pulled out a small knife. He held the knife in his left hand as he approached Butch. He had an evil grin on his face. "Happy Halloween, McPherson. I'm your worst fuckin' nightmare, kid. You're dead!"

Butch had felt a powerful surge of adrenaline as soon as he pocketed the four-leaf clover. He dove and rolled away to his left side quickly when he saw Haynesworth swiping at his little throat with a pocketknife. Haynesworth had missed Butch's throat with the blade by less than an inch. Haynesworth stumbled. Butch got up quickly and whacked Haynesworth in the face with the crowbar. Haynesworth's head began bleeding badly. He dropped to the ground, dazed. He lay there on the patch of grass as Butch bashed his skull in with the crowbar six more times. Haynesworth died quickly. Butch had never felt so powerful in his life. He thought this four-leaf clover he'd recently found in the grass was the main source behind this power.

Butch was breathing heavily from the adrenaline rush. Seconds later, Haynesworth's soul tried to leave his body. The Devil came from beneath the ground, grabbed Haynesworth's soul, and took it deep underground to hell. This happened very quickly, and it was the scariest thing Butch McPherson had ever seen. He jumped back in fear and fled the area. He made it home three minutes later.

When he got back home, his mother was over by the couch next to her husband, crying. Harvard McPherson had just died at the age of 42 from health complications.

DUBLIN
EXPRESS

CHAPTER 3

Thirty years had gone by since the clover theft on the alien planet. It was Halloween night again. Four blue aliens were operating their spaceship and exploring the mysteries of outer space. They needed to find a place to live soon, or they were going to die. They hadn't been able to properly care for the four-leaf clover they'd stolen from the green alien race. The clover was dehydrating. The aliens were surviving on morsels of food and water per day, but their water supply was low.

These blue aliens would run out of their water supply in a month. The same was true of their food supply. Tiny daily drops of a liquid injected into their veins were enough food for them. They originally had brought box loads of this manufactured food on their journey, but they were down to their last box. They needed to find a planet to land on. They'd been searching outer space for a civilized planet and couldn't find one. They passed by Neptune, Saturn, Jupiter, and Mars but found no signs of life anywhere. The blue aliens were wandering for years, looking for another planet out there with life.

The aliens began to pick up life readings from a nearby planet. They were just a few hundred thousand miles from Earth. Seconds later, the electricity in their ship mysteriously failed, and so did their backup generators. The ship went totally black. The only source of light was the shining four-leaf clover. It was incredible and confusing for these curious aliens. They pondered scientific theories in their minds in the darkness of outer space and couldn't come up with any logical theories as to why this happened.

In truth, this magical four-leaf clover took all the electrical energy out of the ship and navigated it on its own. The aliens stood there, staring at the glowing clover as their spaceship took an unknown path. These blue creatures now theorized that this clover had a connection to magic. They were more amazed by this clover than anything they'd ever researched before.

The blue aliens were disoriented. This disorientation suddenly made them all extremely nervous. They were sweating profusely in their battle suits as their heartbeats all sped up. They were unsure if this stolen magical clover was going to kill them or save them.

CHAPTER 4

The blue aliens in the spaceship couldn't handle the intensity of the glowing clover. They were frightened by its green light. The green light around the clover kept blinking on and off. As it did, their spaceship would experience extreme turbulence and rattle uncontrollably.

Soon, the spacecraft reached Earth's atmosphere. Five minutes later, the ship slammed to the ground, and the clover stopped glowing. The blue aliens had crash-landed in a sandpit in the middle of Egypt. Hundreds of Egyptians witnessed this mysterious crash-landing. They surrounded the spaceship with every piece of weaponry they had. Flaming arrows and swords were drawn out in defense and aimed at this spacecraft. The Egyptians were prepared for war.

The four blue aliens were disoriented from the crash landing. Their body suits had protected them from serious harm, but they were still a little shaken from the crash. The aliens all looked at each other and then looked at the clover. They were confused as to how this stolen clover had taken control of their spaceship. One of the aliens grabbed the clover, and they all slowly exited their spacecraft. When one of the aliens stepped on the sand, a flaming arrow was shot at its chest, but it did not damage the alien.

A few more flaming arrows were shot at the aliens, but still, they had no effect. The Egyptians were confused by this. The four aliens began to shoot their laser guns in the air, showing how dangerous their weaponry was. The Egyptians all held their fire and bowed down in respect to these creatures. The blue aliens knew nothing about Earth, but they were more interested in learning from these Egyptians than in going to war with them. The aliens wanted to share their technology. They wanted more answers about the clover. They were now more curious than they had ever been about the clover and what kind of black magic it was capable of.

The aliens were beginning to believe there could be another clover on this planet somewhere. They knew they would need help from these Egyptians if they were ever going to find that clover.

A man had recently died of heart failure, and his body was now in a tomb nearby. In life, this man had been a fearless Egyptian soldier who had taught other soldiers combat skills such as how to construct flaming arrows, sharp swords, and protective shields. The soldier taught them how to build cannons, flaming catapults, and vicious underground traps in the desert. He had also taught them hand-to-hand combat skills, how to spy on areas to gain intelligence on other lands, and how to conquer territory.

The soldier had been resting in the tomb when he started getting chest pains. He began to yell loudly in the middle of a deep sleep. The soldier clasped his hands across his chest tightly and bobbed his head up and down aggressively. He had a vision of a flashing, bright-green four-leaf clover in the middle of a spaceship, with four blue aliens around it. Then, the soldier died in the tomb on Halloween night.

The Egyptians had been devastated when their famous leader died. Now, many of the Egyptians were beginning to believe these strange blue aliens had come here to bring their famous leader back to life. The Egyptians showed the creatures the soldier's tomb. The aliens looked down at the soldier and then looked at each other. They were coming up with ideas. The Egyptians kept pointing to the soldier's heart, showing where they believed his mysterious death had originated.

The blue aliens began operating on the soldier. One of them began rubbing an ointment on the soldier's chest. The blue alien species had created this ointment in a lab on their home planet and it was designed to decrease blood flow during autopsies. The aliens began cutting through the soldier's skin with a mini-laser. A crowd of Egyptians stood nearby while the autopsy was being performed. They were amazed at how advanced these blue creatures were with medical technology.

A few minutes into the autopsy, the aliens had to stop when they noticed something very strange. The soldier's heart was black. The blue aliens were puzzled by this. They were expecting the color of the heart to be red. This went beyond the logic of medical theories of their alien anatomy. They were wondering why the color of this soldier's heart was black. A few of the Egyptians peeked over while the aliens performed the autopsy and were completely puzzled by the color of the heart. It was a mystery to all who witnessed it.

The blue aliens looked at each other for a brief moment. One of them had the clover on hand. The alien pointed to the soldier's heart, then put the clover near it. The blue aliens all looked at each other again. They continued the autopsy. They exposed the soldier's entire heart. They rubbed some more ointment around the soldier's black heart and began slowly taking small lasers to the black heart. They attached the four-leaf clover to the soldier's black heart, then began to seal the soldier's heart back together with multiple layers of white cloth. A few minor black bloodstains oozed through the cloth.

The crowd of Egyptians and the aliens kept staring at the soldier in the tomb after the autopsy was finished. They were all wondering what would happen next. A few minutes passed. All of a sudden, the soldier roared loudly, then fell silent and motionless. The soldier had turned into a mummy due to the magical power from the four-leaf clover implanted in the mummy's heart. The aliens and the Egyptians were amazed by this, wondering if the mummy would come back to life again. The aliens and the Egyptians waited for signs of life, but there were none. The mummy appeared dead again. It was now midnight. Halloween had ended.

CHAPTER 5

A year passed. It was Halloween morning. The Egyptians and the four blue aliens watched the mummy in the tomb closely for body movement. They had preserved the mummy's body in a tomb. The Egyptians and the aliens believed the mummy might come back from the dead. There were no signs of life. Frustration set in for these blue creatures and Egyptians; however, they continued to remain patient and keep a close eye on the mummy as the hours passed.

The wind blew a little bit stronger in the Egyptian desert, spreading sand all around the tomb. The sun began to sink slightly, and the sky had darkened. Suddenly, the mummy began to twitch. The Egyptians and the aliens gazed at the mummy, eyes wide open, anxious to see more movement. The mummy began to bob its head back and forth.

Then it yelled, "I'm alive!"

Slowly, it lifted its body upright and got out of the tomb. The mummy attempted to walk, but it had no leg strength and began to wobble. Three Egyptians held the mummy upright and made sure it didn't fall. The mummy looked around at its followers. It noticed four blue creatures standing nearby and observing. This triggered a memory of the strange vision it had before dying—of the four blue aliens in a spaceship, surrounded by a glowing four-leaf clover.

The mummy felt its heart slowly beating. It clutched at its heart and groaned in pain. Its live body was slowly adapting to its repaired heart, but it needed more rest. The Egyptians carefully placed the mummy in the tomb to rest. The Egyptians and the aliens were beginning to see signs of life in this mummy, but they wanted the mummy to become as deadly as it was in its past life. The mummy slept for three hours with the others gazing at it the whole time. Then it woke up and roared again. Suddenly, it got up from its tomb and walked around the room. The Egyptians were nearby to make sure the mummy didn't wobble on its legs again.

The mummy managed to walk across the room and step outside on the sand. It remembered the area where it taught combat training skills to the Egyptians, and it walked to a training battlefield located a few hundred feet behind the tomb. The area was fenced in. The mummy opened the door and entered the battlefield. It looked around at all its weaponry. The aliens and the Egyptians followed the mummy to the battlefield. Finally, it spoke.

"Men, my heart has been repaired, so I came back to life. I can feel something evil inside of me. I don't know who the fuck these blue creatures are or why they came here, but I know it was them who saved me. My eyes began to open, and I saw them working on my heart. This is a miracle. I can still fulfill my destiny to conquer other lands. I'll need your help. These blue creatures are geniuses. And I'll need their help as well. Their battle suits are well constructed. Show them our weapons, and let them show you more of their weaponry. I trained you soldiers for this, and I'm grateful I'll be able to carry out this evil quest. I want the combat training facility to be used. I want pyramids built in front of my tomb. I want warships built. We'll set sail with many soldiers in these warships and attack other lands on Halloween night. Use your training skills to spy on these other lands so we can be more prepared for these attacks. I know there is another one of these clovers out there somewhere on this earth. I can feel it. We must find it! Next Halloween, we'll strike!"

The mummy then dropped dead, out of energy. The aliens quickly came to its aid. One of the aliens began working on bringing the mummy back up to strength. This procedure failed. However, the Egyptians had all they needed for now. They had listened to what their evil leader had to say before it died. The Egyptians and the aliens now knew the mummy was becoming stronger and slowly adapting to its evil heart. Next year, on Halloween, they would strike India.

CHAPTER 6

The next year, on Halloween, 5,000 combat-trained Egyptian soldiers, four blue aliens, and the mummy were moments away from an invasion of India. The Egyptian soldiers had spent the past year spying on their land, learning a lot about the geographical landscape of the country. One of the blue aliens drew a picture of a four-leaf clover on the face of a rock to motivate the army to find this rare artifact.

The Egyptians were prepared to wipe the Indian soldiers out, and they did so. With the help of the four blue aliens safeguarding the mummy's heart, this army was very dangerous. The Indian soldiers kept shooting arrows at the aliens, but they inflicted no damage. They threw small axes at the blue aliens, but the axes were completely useless against their battle suits.

Halloween ended in a complete bloodbath of hell for these unprepared Indian soldiers—3,458 Indian soldiers lost their lives in the Halloween attack. Only 345 Egyptian soldiers were killed in the battle against India.

The next year, on Halloween, more Egyptian soldiers joined this powerful army. They had 5,500 Egyptian soldiers ready to raid southern Africa. Many African countries were demolished. They shot arrows at the aliens and pondered why their direct hits to these aliens' chests did no damage. The aliens' battle suits were the most inventive weaponry that the southern African armies had ever seen.

A year later, on Halloween, Jamaica was raided and defeated by this ruthless Egyptian army.

A decade later, this Egyptian army had wiped out nearly half of the entire population on Earth. Many Egyptian soldiers died during these attacks. South America, North America, and most of Europe were destroyed by the Egyptians. The Egyptians still hadn't found the other four-leaf clover, however.

For the past year, Egyptian soldiers had been spying on the Irish, but the Irish people were not aware of this. Egyptian war spies got to know the coastline of Dublin. Ten Egyptian soldiers searched Dublin's terrain and became familiar with the steep hills in the woods. They became aware of a waterfall near the Dublin River. They noticed that two defense towers were being built next to a battlement near the waterfall. A local construction crew had built the battlement and the defense towers out of stone pillars.

It took thirty Irishmen six months to complete this Irish war trap. The Irishman worked very long and hard—twelve-hour days every day, regardless of the weather. The battlement was fully constructed a week ago. The Egyptians knew the Irish were protecting something important to go through all this trouble to build a battlement in this very location.

Halloween was two days away. The dangerous Egyptian army was waiting in four warships twenty miles upriver from where these defense towers were located. One thousand Egyptians, the four blue aliens, and the mummy were waiting for Halloween night to come so they could wage war on Ireland.

CHAPTER 7

One day had passed. It was October 30th. Carnival workers were setting up food shacks and carnival games for the local Dublin Halloween Fair. Many Dublin locals were planning to attend the festivity.

In a different section of Dublin, a construction crew had just finished a ten-year project that consisted of digging tunnels and setting deadly traps inside a cave. The traps were designed to catch invaders completely off-guard and make them appear as if they were never even there. The name of this construction company was Patrician Construction, and it was the most efficient building crew in all of Ireland. A 45-year-old man named David Patrician owned the company. David had a family. He had a wife named Maureen and a two-year-old son named Declan. His wife was forty-one years old. About ten years ago, they met each other for the first time at the Dublin River. They both happened to be fishing near each other on the banks of the river that day. They talked for a few hours while they fished. They were interested in each other, so they made plans to meet up at the Dublin River and go fishing. Their friendship soon turned into a relationship. About four years ago, David and Maureen got engaged. They have been married for a little over three years and they own a house. Their house was about a five-minute walk from the cave. Maureen was at home taking care of their son. David still had to take care of a few things on the job before heading home.

The construction crew had spent many long days developing passageways in this cave.

The purpose of all these tunnels and barricades was protection from enemies in a time of war. Mr. Patrician didn't believe this was entirely necessary, considering things had been peaceful in Ireland for many years. He believed that having Irish soldiers trained to defend their land was all the Irish townspeople needed to feel safe.

Butch McPherson was now a 50-year-old man. He was Mr. Patrician's business partner. Butch had convinced his partner to help him turn the cave into a battleground. Mr. Patrician had agreed to build this project with Butch and three other Irishmen for $10,000. The cost was broken down to $1,000 per year. Butch agreed to give David half the money upfront and the other half of the money upon completion of the project.

Ten years back, on October 1, Butch gave David $5,000. Butch would not have had the funds for this had it not been for the $100 he'd stolen from the Dublin Express Bakery when he was a six-year-old boy. He'd used some of that stolen money to help support him and his mother after the tragic death of his father. Butch had then saved up the $5,000 to fund half of the cave operation by working many jobs, such as a fisherman and a laborer. Butch McPherson was also a trained army soldier. He still had his lucky four-leaf clover, which he kept in a satchel and carried with him at all times.

He'd convinced the Irish army to construct defense towers near the Dublin River in case the land was ever attacked. The leader of the army liked the idea and signed off on the project. The leader of this army was named Connor McArthur, and he was the same age as Butch. Butch only wanted these towers built for an extra layer of security protecting his cave project. Butch and Connor had known each other for twenty years. Connor knew Butch was serious about his cave operation.

Connor had helped Butch with some of the cave construction over the past ten years. He knew Butch had mainly recommended that the towers be constructed nearby to protect his cave. Connor also realized that, if attackers ever invaded Dublin's territory by way of the sea, building the battlement and the two defense towers just offshore of the Dublin River near the cave and the waterfall was strategically sound.

Even if the cave project didn't exist, a battlement still would have been constructed. Mr. McPherson had a lot of say in where the battlement was built. He had helped with a small portion of this project. He spent most of his days and many long nights constructing the traps and getting to know ways of maneuvering around the dangerous cave safely. His crew knew the layout of the caves as well, but Butch had a better sense of direction than all these men. Butch walked in certain sections of this dark cave many times, over and over again, at night when the crew members were resting after a long day's work. This helped Butch get to know this cave better than all his crew.

Butch had a defense plan if his land was ever attacked. This plan was to barricade himself at the end of the cave and protect his lucky four-leaf clover from invaders. He knew that someday, an invading army would come after the clover. What Butch didn't know was that a second four-leaf clover existed.

CHAPTER 8

David and Butch were standing in the cave, piling up construction equipment. They'd just finished grabbing a few wheelbarrows and shovels and placing them in an emergency supply room that had been built in the cave. David and Butch were in the supply room, and David had a few questions to ask his partner.

David said, "So Butch, this cave project has finally been completed. It took a little over ten years, but finally, it's done. I must say, it's a great war strategy design because we know how to move around in these areas and our enemies won't. That's how we'll defend our land, should the occasion ever arise."

"I taught you well, David. I'm glad I was able to ingrain this idea in your mind after all these years. Of course, that's why we'll win the battle if one presents itself. Our enemies will fall victim to our death traps. And, of course, my lucky four-leaf clover will play a major role in our victory."

"What is it with you and that fuckin' clover, McPherson? Why do you think it's so goddamn special anyways?"

"It's always guided me when I've been in trouble, and that's all you need to know."

"Have you ever thought to think that the fuckin' thing could possibly be bringing you trouble instead? Like a curse or something?"

"A curse? That's ridiculous, David. My magical clover isn't capable of producing any curses. It's not that kind of clover. It brings me good karma."

"Well, I got news for you, my friend, good karma and bad karma both exist. Don't let this precious little clover of yours make you too superstitious. Why don't we just stop talking about this silly clover? This project has me wiped out, so I'm taking the day off tomorrow, getting drunk, and going to the Halloween Fair. But, before this bender, I'd like the $5,000 you owe me now that the cave project is under wraps."

"Well, about that other $5,000, Patrician, you see, the funny little thing about that is, I don't have it."

"What the fuck do you mean you don't have it? I've been letting you get away without paying for the other half of this project for a fuckin' decade. You told me that the money wasn't going to be a problem. This sounds like a huge fuckin' problem to me. How the fuck am I going to pay my crew members this week?"

David shoved Butch a little bit. David felt like punching his friend over this cash dispute.

"Relax, David. You're the best fuckin' architect in all of Ireland. You told me yourself you have $20,000 saved."

"Yes, I do, asshole. But that's not the fuckin' point. You told me you had the money, and you lied to me and fucked me over instead. I have extra money to spare and pay my employees with, but that cash is supposed to be used for my own family and my construction business."

"Exactly, David. That money is for your construction business, so use it for that and pay the other three cave diggers," said McPherson with a smirk on his face.

"You wipe that fuckin' smirk off your face right now, McPherson. This bullshit isn't funny. I could have been building more schools and hospitals for the community. Instead, I've been helping you with your war traps when there isn't even a goddamn war. The fuckin' sacrifice that I made helping you build this barricade, and you don't even have the $5,000 cash you promised me. It's good to know what a $5,000 cash promise from Butch McPherson is worth. It isn't worth shit!"

"David, please try to understand that this project was necessary."

"What about the payment for the fuckin' project, McPherson? That's necessary as well, and you fucked me on it. You know, what I want in return is that precious little four-leaf clover of yours. Give it to me right now before I beat the living fuck out of you!"

"David, you have every right to be upset. But I can't give you my lucky clover."

"Then what else do you got to offer me, McPherson?"

"I'll sign the deed to my house over to you the first thing in the morning."

"Your house is a small little shithole that's worth no more than $2,500."

"The place just needs a little fixing up. You're an architect. That kind of shit is right up your alley."

"But that's only half of the money. What about the other half, you fuckin' scumbag?"

"I'll work for you for free, for two hours a day, every day, for the next five years if you agree to take off $500 a year from my debt to you. I would need to go back to being a fisherman to earn cash that I'll still need, but I'll be fishing nearby on the Dublin River, and I promise you I'll pay back my debt."

"I'll agree to this, McPherson, because I'm your partner." David forcefully pointed a finger at his conniving friend. "But if you fuck me over in any way just once more, this friendship, this partnership, and your life will all come to a crushing end. You got it?"

"All right, David. I got it. Now stop pointing your fuckin' finger at me and try to relax. You'll live longer. Sounds like you could use a drink tonight. Let's go to the Dublin Brewery, buddy. I'm buying."

"I don't want to see your face anymore tonight, McPherson. I want the deed to your house signed over to me first thing in the morning. I'll know where to find you if you ever fuck me over again."

"You can come find me at the end of the cave. My new home."

"I must say, McPherson, you're one fucked-up individual. I'm getting the fuck out of here. I'll see you first thing in the morning."

"Ok, David. Just go home and get some rest."

"Don't tell me what to do, McPherson."

David Patrician left the cave and headed home.

Butch yelled out to his other three coworkers, "Gentlemen! Could you all please come over to the emergency supply room? I have something to say."

Kilgore, Garrison, and Ferguson hovering around a candle in the dark nearby, stopped their three-way conversation and headed over to the supply room.

Butch said, "Gentlemen, thank you all for your hard work and dedication in the completion of this project. It wasn't easy digging out these tunnels and passageways inside the cave. It took strenuous effort from all of you, and Mr. Patrician will pay you the money he promised you for this week tomorrow afternoon. I know you were all supposed to get paid today, but, unfortunately, there was a minor misunderstanding with the company budget that's currently being handled as we speak. I apologize for the payment delay, but just remain patient until tomorrow afternoon, and David and I will have your money. How about we head downtown to the Dublin Brewery and celebrate a job well done?"

Ferguson replied, "We don't feel like drinking with you right now, McPherson. We're all pissed off about not getting paid today. This is fuckin' bullshit."

Kilgore and Garrison agreed. The three men looked at McPherson like he was the biggest scumbag on earth. A few moments later, they left the emergency supply room, exited the cave, and headed back to their homes. It was 10:00 p.m. They left McPherson all alone in the emergency supply room. Butch McPherson just smirked and shook his head.

Butch didn't feel like going home and spending his last night in his house. He felt like sleeping in the emergency supply room tonight. He had a strange obsession with this cave. He grabbed a bottle of whiskey he'd stashed on a shelf above five metal shovels.

"Cheers to my new home," he said to himself. He took a few sips from the whiskey bottle. He was happy to be alone in his new home. Butch soon became tired and dozed off.

The clock struck midnight.

It was now Halloween. A fisherman named Montgomery Walsh was heading upriver in a small fishing boat. The fisherman had just passed the four Egyptian warships when a strong wind gust came and the river began to get rough and choppy. The fisherman was a rugged man with a scruffy beard—and he was a sociopath. He was pure evil and capable of murder, having killed eight people. The fisherman had collected all his eight victims' heads and kept them as trophies. The fisherman used a small fishing knife on all his victims. The fisherman sneak-attacked them, then went in for the kill.

All the victims were innocent people who were fishing. The fisherman was an expert at blindside kills. He was also an expert at fleeing from a murder scene without a trace. All these murders had occurred on Halloween over the timespan of a decade. The authorities had no leads or witnesses to these horrific Halloween murders. Many people in Dublin and other small towns nearby feared the mysterious Halloween killer.

The fisherman neared the battlement. He docked his small fishing boat off the river in a shallow, muddy area. He stepped out of his fishing boat and climbed up ten feet of jagged rocks. He looked at the battlement and the defense towers. Nobody was anywhere in sight. He kept roaming this area of Dublin. The fisherman had a small knife in his right hand. He was looking for an innocent victim to stalk and then kill. He walked near the cave and noticed a raccoon crawl into a crevice. The fisherman realized the gap was an entryway into a dark and mysterious cavern.

The fisherman entered the cave. He slowly wiggled through a few narrow sections and made it completely through in about thirty seconds. The Fisherman began to slowly creep around in the dark cave, his knife held out in his right hand. He walked around in this cave and saw two different paths. There was a path straight ahead of him and a path to the right. The fisherman took the path to the right.

He walked thirty feet down this path. The path ended. There was nothing but rocks blocking the way ahead. However, to the left side of these rocks was the entryway to the emergency supply room. The fisherman peeked his head inside and noticed a man was sleeping. He saw the man slightly rolling around on the ground in the room. The fisherman took slow and quiet steps. He slowly crept up to the man.

The fisherman took a vicious swipe at Butch's throat with his fishing knife, but Butch had awoken. He was having a terrible nightmare about a fisherman who snuck into his cave and tried to kill him. Butch's nightmare had become a reality.

Butch screamed. As the clock struck midnight on Halloween, his nightmare and the fisherman's movements occurred at the same time. Butch's magical clover had given him supernatural visions of the fisherman's actions and allowed him to wake up when his life was in danger. When Butch woke up from this horrific nightmare and noticed an evil man attacking him with a knife, he had little time to defend himself.

The fisherman took a vicious knife swipe at McPherson's throat with his right hand. Butch McPherson used his supernatural reflexes to block the knife from cutting his throat, grabbing the fisherman's right arm quickly with both of his hands. The fisherman dropped his knife and grunted in anger at his failure. The fisherman punched McPherson in the face a few times and began to strangle him. Bleeding from his nose, McPherson shook around and struggled to breathe. As McPherson desperately tried to fight off the fisherman's strong chokehold, he looked over to his right and could see the fisherman's knife on the ground about four feet away from him.

McPherson reached his right hand out and grabbed the fisherman's knife. He swung the knife at the fisherman's throat.

"Ah!" groaned the fisherman. The fisherman's chokehold became less forceful almost instantly after being stabbed in the throat. Blood poured down his chest.

Within a few seconds, the fisherman dropped to the ground and died. McPherson stood up quickly and looked down at the fisherman. Without hesitation, McPherson yelled out, "Die, you fuckin' bastard!" as he stabbed the fisherman in the throat a few more times. McPherson's body was flowing with adrenaline. He knew his lucky, Irish, four-leaf clover had saved his life. He knew the clover had awoken him at just the right time to save his life.

McPherson pocketed the fisherman's bloody knife. He looked at his victim. He lit a candle in the room to get a closer look at this evil man's face. He'd never seen this man before. He had a strange feeling that the man who had just tried to kill him was the mysterious Halloween killer. McPherson was a very private person. He didn't want anyone to know this had happened. The fisherman intruding on him and making an attempt to kill him had McPherson on edge. He just wanted to get rid of the body.

McPherson dragged the man's body down a passageway about a quarter of a mile long. The passageway led to a dead end in the cave that had a giant hole, which McPherson and his crew had dug out. The hole was a 300-foot drop into a deeper section of ground. When McPherson reached the end of the passageway, he took one last look at the fisherman.

"So long, asshole," said McPherson as he shoved this mysterious man's body down into the deep hole. The fisherman's body dropped down, and McPherson heard a giant *thud* when the body hit the ground.

McPherson headed back to the emergency supply room. He arrived there five minutes later. He grabbed a sword. He stood guard in the emergency supply room with a sword drawn, prepared to defend himself. He stayed up most of the night, ready to defend his cave. He finally dosed off around seven-thirty in the morning.

CHAPTER 9

It was 8:00 a.m., Halloween morning. Carnival workers were setting up their booths, getting ready for the Dublin Halloween Fair. There were security guards on duty for the fair. Seventy-five men and women were on security shift. There were 333 people walking around the Halloween Fair and waiting for the booths to open up shop in a little less than an hour. More people were planning to attend the Dublin Halloween Fair.

A 54-year-old farmer named Paul O'Sullivan was setting up his booth. Paul was a cockeyed, in-bred farmer who cultivated a small garden in the Dublin Woods. He had been a farmer his whole life. He kept a scarecrow in his garden to keep the crows away. He worshipped this scarecrow and believed it was sacred. Paul had made the scarecrow on Halloween when he was a six-year-old boy, and he'd cherished this handcrafted prop ever since. Paul had a scruffy brown beard and wore dirty overalls all the time. He was missing many teeth due to poor hygiene and from getting involved in a few scuffles in the past, which he'd lost. His nose was warped.

Paul had stability issues. He was overprotective of his garden. He was very uptight about others touching his crops. He kept his inventory behind his booth. He didn't allow potential customers to touch his vegetables. Paul thought other people had dirty hands, despite his own hands being filthy. He didn't wash his hands much, and they were always covered in dirt. He had a few cuts and blisters on his hands as a result of working many long hours in his garden. His hands had developed damage in his joints, nerves, and bones from years of being a farmer. He had a crippling arthritis in both of his hands.

He'd been setting up his vegetable booth for the last ten minutes. He was stocking shelves behind his booth with vegetables. He had potatoes, tomatoes, corn, and carrots on display for sale.

While he was getting set up for the fair, two young Irish hooligans started distracting him. These kids were running around near his booth and annoying him. Their names were Daniel Fitzpatrick and Heath McManis. They were both eight years old, and they were best friends. They lived a few houses over from each other. They were at the fair unaccompanied by their parents. They were running around, giggling, and playing tag near Paul's booth, and Paul didn't like this.

"Hey, cut the shit, you damn hooligans!" shouted Paul at these two kids. The kids didn't listen to the angry farmer. They just kept playing their game near his booth.

"What do you got, shit for brains? Get the hell away from my booth, you damn hooligans!" Paul shouted again. The kids stopped playing tag after Paul's second stern warning. But they decided to stick around near Paul's booth and continue to annoy him. Paul tried his best to ignore these kids and continued to stock his vegetables on the shelves behind his booth. When Paul was in the middle of stocking his tomatoes, both kids wandered behind his booth.

"Hey, Mister, do you need any help back here?" asked Daniel. Paul turned around and became furious at these two kids.

"No! I don't need any fuckin' help! Get the hell out of my booth, you damn hooligans," shouted Paul.

"Hey, Mister, you need to relax," Heath said. "You're way too tense right now. It's Halloween. Try to have some fun today."

O'Sullivan didn't respond. He just became more enraged. He shook his head in frustration, shooed the children away with his hands, then went back to work. The kids walked away from his booth and left the area for a few minutes. They walked across the street and watched a drunken clown set up his balloon booth. They saw a homeless bum passed out on the sidewalk. There were many other carnival workers and people around the area.

A police officer named Arthur Jones walked by and noticed these kids approaching the clown. He also noticed the clown looked a little drunk. Before these kids made their way over to the clown, the police officer walked up to Daniel and Heath and said, "Come on, kids, the clown is very busy getting ready for the fair today. Go play across the street, and don't bother him."

The two kids didn't respond to the officer. But they listened to him and walked back across the street. Officer Jones then continued to walk around the fair, keeping an eye on things.

The kids went back over to Paul's booth. They both went behind the booth. "Hey, Mister, let me try one of these tomatoes," said Heath. He reached his right hand over the vegetable display booth and grabbed a tomato.

O'Sullivan grunted in anger. "Don't touch my tomaters, you damn hooligan!" he shouted.

Heath got nervous and dropped the tomato on the ground near the booth. Daniel and Heath both began to fear this angry farmer. They both fled from the booth. O'Sullivan had a pitchfork behind his booth. He grabbed his pitchfork and chased after these two kids. People at the fair soon became aware of the chaos. O'Sullivan made it about ten feet out of his booth when angry fairgoers went vigilante on him. O'Sullivan dropped his pitchfork as two grown men tackled him to the ground.

These two men pinned O'Sullivan down to the pavement and began to beat him. They restrained O'Sullivan and began throwing punches at his face. O'Sullivan started to bleed from his nose and mouth. A few of his teeth were punched out by these two vigilantes. O'Sullivan coughed. Then he spat out blood and three broken teeth out of his mouth. Soon after, more angry fairgoers joined in on the beating. Five more men, and a few women, got involved in the beating of the farmer. The vigilantes rushed toward him and started punching and kicking him. The farmer yelled, "Ah! Ah! Get the fuck off me! Ah! Ah!"

The Irish vigilantes continued to beat and restrain the farmer. Twenty seconds later, Officer Jones rushed over to the mob scene and tried to calm down the angry vigilantes. Some of the vigilantes stopped beating the farmer as they backed off and let the officer do his job. Some of the vigilantes were still beating the shit out of the farmer while Officer Jones tried to control the chaos.

A few more officers arrived on the scene about a minute later. The officers rushed over to the area when they'd seen and heard the chaos in the distance. The officers were trying to keep the riled-up vigilantes under control. The officers were standing around the beaten farmer, trying to protect him from the vigilantes. O'Sullivan was dazed from the beating. He had a concussion. He spat out more blood from his mouth as he lay on the pavement, injured.

"They punched out my damn teeth," said O'Sullivan.

"Nobody here gives a shit about your broken teeth," replied Officer Jones. "And you won't be selling your precious vegetables today either. Come on, shithead. Get up."

Officer Jones forcefully pulled O'Sullivan up off the pavement. "Put your hands behind your back. You're under arrest, asshole," said Officer Jones. O'Sullivan was in a state of confusion. He was very dizzy. He had difficulty standing up. He wobbled around on his feet as he stood there, completely dazed. "I said put your fuckin' hands behind your fuckin' back, now asshole!" said Officer Jones. O'Sullivan grunted in pain and put his hands behind his back. Officer Jones placed O'Sullivan in handcuffs. Officer Jones was very forceful with O'Sullivan and he placed the handcuffs tight around O'Sullivan's wrists. "These fuckin' handcuffs are too damn tight. They're cutting off the fuckin' circulation to my fuckin' hands," said O'Sullivan.

"Too fuckin' bad, asshole," said Officer Jones. "The fuckin' handcuffs will be off your wrists in just a minute, once your sorry in-bred ass is safely locked away for the day. Come on, buddy. Let's go."

O'Sullivan held his head down in shame. Soon after, the vigilantes had calmed down, and the situation was resolved. A few hundred people at the fair had witnessed this chaos. The officers took the beaten man away from the area. Paul O'Sullivan was arrested for disorderly conduct and placed in a holding cell for the day. Officer Jones removed the handcuffs off of O'Sullivan's wrists once he was placed in the cell. He tucked the handcuffs in the back of his police uniform. Officer Jones walked out of the holding cell. He turned around and looked at O'Sullivan. "You can stay in here for the day and think about what you've done, you fuckin' scumbag," said Officer Jones.

"Fuck you, buddy!"

"Fuck you, as well. As a matter of fact, why don't you go fuck yourself while you rot in here for the day, you piece of fuckin' shit," said Officer Jones as he shut the door and locked it. Officer Jones spat on the ground and went back to business. O'Sullivan's vegetable booth was shut down by the security guards at the fair.

Heath and Daniel continued running away from the fair. Nobody at the fair decided to stop them. Heath and Daniel ran down the block and cut through a few side streets nearby. Their houses were five minutes away from the fair. Five minutes later, they had both made it back to their houses. Heath and Daniel stayed home for the remainder of the day after the mischief they'd caused at the Halloween Fair.

It was now 8:20 a.m. The Egyptian mummy had just awoken. It had learned to wake up early in the morning so it could create more destruction on Halloween. The four blue aliens were by its side. It looked at the aliens and then got out of its tomb. The mummy walked outside and onto the deck of the warship and looked down at a few hundred Egyptians on the lower deck of the boat. The Egyptians bowed down to their evil leader.

The mummy said, "Today we're going to make history. We're going to rule over a new land and repopulate it with Egyptians. I believe this land is known as Dublin, Ireland, but it won't be for long. I want to call this land New Egypt once we're through wiping out their unprepared army tonight. The Irish soldiers won't know how to kill the blue aliens because of their weaponry. These fuckin' aliens are going to blast the hell out of these Irish pussies with their laser guns. We're going to wage war and crush these Irish soldiers. I must say there really is something unique about this land, more than any other land we've conquered. This terrain is very green.

The second clover is somewhere on this land. I can feel it in my evil heart. Our men have scoped out this terrain covertly over the last year. We're all prepared to march as one army and kill anyone Irish. They won't stand a chance against our unstoppable army. We'll win this fight and take what belongs to us. We'll find what belongs to me—the other four-leaf clover! This is why we go to war, gentlemen. The war boats will set sail down the Dublin River, and we'll begin our invasion!"

The Egyptian soldiers cheered for their evil leader. They were prepared to set sail down the Dublin River and strike. The four blue aliens and the mummy were ready to wage war on Ireland and show no mercy in their hunt for the other four-leaf clover. The Irish were about to be ambushed.

CHAPTER 10

General Butch McPherson had just woken up. He'd fallen asleep on the floor in the emergency supply room. He was hungover; the whiskey had taken a bit of a toll on him last night. The self-defense murder was also messing with his mind. He was very grateful he had his lucky Irish four-leaf clover with him last night when he was attacked. Despite all that had happened, he knew he had to deal with his business with Mr. Patrician. He left the supply room, exited the cave, and headed to his house to grab the deed. He had a little over a half-hour walk to get to his house.

***

Meanwhile, it was now 9:00 a.m., and the Dublin Halloween Fair had just gotten underway. A drunken clown named Mickey Randle was selling balloons at the fair. Mickey was stumbling all over the place. The fair had been open for 10 minutes, and no one would buy a balloon from this man. He was just way too drunk. The clown wore green shoes with a green suit and wig. He had issues with alcohol.

Many of the fairgoers were disgusted with how drunk this clown was. "Balloons, here! Get your balloons here! Two balloons for the price of one, from now until 10:00 a.m. Take advantage of this tremendous bargain, folks! Balloon, anyone?" said Mickey as he slurred his speech. A drunk, ten-year-old child named Benjamin Green was at the fair all by himself, walking around near Mickey's balloon booth. Benjamin lived right around the corner of the fair. Benjamin had busted into his parent's liquor cabinet ten minutes ago, while his parents were sleeping, and guzzled a half pint of rum. He just left his house a few minutes ago and headed to the fair. The wild kid just wanted to have a good buzz on, while attending the fair today. "Hey kid, you wanna buy a fuckin' balloon from your good old pal, Mickey?" said the clown to this drunken child. Benjamin looked at Mickey and gave him the finger. "Show some respect, you little fart-nose, chicken-shit, fuckin' wimp," said Mickey. The drunken kid just looked at Mickey like he was a fuckin' joke and walked away. Two security guards at the fair were standing nearby and had heard what the clown had said to this drunken child. The two security guards did not like what Mickey had said to this kid. The two security guards walked over to the balloon booth and approached Mickey the clown. These two security guards were new to the staff. It was their first day ever working a security shift. Officers Burnes and Nolan were 18 years old. They both did volunteer work for Connor McArthur's battlement project and, in return, Connor had agreed to hire and train these two young, arrogant kids how to become disciplined officers.

He had plans for these two to become soldiers. They would be responsible for fortressing his battlement. They just were not trained enough to be at that level yet. With Connor McArthur vouching for these two young men, they were able to land jobs as local security officers. The city of Dublin needed extra security for today, and these two young officers went over to the clown to calm him down.

Officer Burnes said to Mickey the clown, "Hey, buddy, no one here wants to buy a fuckin' balloon from you because you're shitfaced. Both of us heard that smart-ass remark you just made to that little kid. It was very disrespectful of you to say something like that to an innocent kid. We can't have people like you fuckin' up the fair for the rest of the fairgoers. I'm going to have to ask you to shut down this shitty balloon operation right now and leave the fair without incident. Got it, you fuckin' cornball?"

"I'm not going anywhere, asshole. I'm staying right here at my balloon booth. So, if you don't mind stepping aside, I've got business to attend to. Good day, gentlemen."

Officer Nolan became angry with the clown's disrespect for local authority. He took control into his own hands. "That's it, you fuckin' screwball! I've had enough of your bullshit," shouted Officer Nolan as he pulled out a baton and clubbed Mickey in the face with it. The drunken clown stumbled and then fell to the pavement. Officer Nolan let loose on the clown and clubbed his body repeatedly until he was unconscious. Officer Burnes placed the clown in handcuffs. The clown had a bruised ribcage and a broken jaw. Blood was dripping from the clown's mouth. Fairgoers were staring at this chaos.

Officer Nolan made a brief announcement to the fairgoers, "It's all right, folks. The situation has been handled, and the clown is safely in custody. Tell you what, if you want some balloons, Mickey here said he was giving them all away, so feel free to take a few of them off his booth. Sorry about any inconvenience this has caused. Enjoy the rest of your day."

Some of the fairgoers grabbed a few free balloons for their children. Burnes and Nolan pulled the clown up and walked him to a private security area at the fair. When they were walking the beaten clown to the security facility, something awful started to happen. The Egyptians docked their four warships near a giant pier a few blocks around the corner from the Dublin Halloween Fair. They began to exit the warships and raid the Dublin Halloween Fair.

CHAPTER 11

The Dublin Halloween Fair was under attack. It was 9:06 a.m. The Egyptians were killing whoever was Irish. Security officers were getting shot in the chest with flaming arrows. Little children and their families were getting slaughtered with swords by ruthless Egyptians. The blue aliens were shooting lasers at the fairgoers. They surrounded the mummy to safeguard its evil heart.

A few Irish security officers pulled out their batons and clubbed the aliens, but their battle suits protected them. Officer Jones crept up behind one of the blue aliens and began clubbing the alien in the back of the head with his baton, but the blue alien was not harmed by his attacks. The blue alien turned around and blasted Officer Jones directly in the chest with a laser shot. Officer Jones dropped to the ground and died immediately. He was 43 years old. The other security guards began to run for their lives after their baton strikes to these dangerous blue aliens did no damage. The security officers got shot with laser guns and killed.

An Irishman named Joseph Kerrigan was playing a ring toss game when the fair was raided. Instead of running for his life, Joseph Kerrigan decided to fight back and defend his Irish homeland. Kerrigan picked up a cinderblock. The cinderblock was on the pavement near the ring toss game. He crept up behind an Egyptian soldier who aimed a flaming arrow at a crowd of Irish people who were fleeing from the Halloween Fair. Kerrigan cracked the Egyptian soldier in the back of the skull with the cinderblock.

The Egyptian soldier dropped his bow and his flaming arrow as he buckled to his knees and fell to the pavement, completely dazed. The Egyptian soldier lay on the pavement with a head injury. The Egyptian soldier groaned in pain. Experiencing internal bleeding, his eyes rolled around uncontrollably. Blood drooled out of the Egyptian soldier's mouth and dripped out of the back of his skull. A crowd of escaping Irish people then stomped on the defenseless Egyptian soldier. The Egyptian soldier died soon after being stomped on by the fleeing Irish folks.

An Egyptian soldier with a sword in his hand crept behind 30-year-old Joseph Kerrigan and beheaded him. A few fairgoers killed some of the Egyptian soldiers, but, soon after, more Egyptian soldiers swarmed them and killed them with swords. It was complete chaos.

Mickey the clown snapped out of it. The fair being raided caused a major distraction for Burnes and Nolan. Burnes, Nolan, and the clown were right next to the door of the security room.

Officer Nolan said, "The Halloween Fair is under attack. We all have to hide in here until we're safe."

"Not me, asshole," said Mickey the clown. He lunged aggressively and began to strangle Officer Nolan with his handcuffs. Officer Burnes tried to help his fellow officer and free him from the clown's vicious chokehold. Officer Burnes tried to club the clown in the jaw. The clown leaned forward very quickly and took a deep bite out of the side of Officer Burnes's neck. Officer Burnes yelled out in agony and shook in pain.

Mickey bit Officer Burnes's neck while also choking Officer Nolan with the handcuffs. Soon after, both officers fell to the ground and died. Mickey grabbed the key out of Officer Burnes's pocket and uncuffed himself. An Irishman who had witnessed this approached Mickey to try to tackle him. Mickey moved out of the way of the tackle and managed to pin the Irishman to the ground, then bashed the man's skull into the pavement three times, and the man died.

Mickey then approached the mob. He found a sword on the ground and picked it up. The sword had been dropped by an Egyptian soldier when he was killed in battle. Mickey killed a few Egyptian soldiers nearby, then a few Irish folks. Mickey was in this war for himself. It took a mob of Irish fairgoers to finally put his killing spree to an end. The Irish vigilantes beat the shit out of this clown. Mickey Randle died from injuries nearly a minute after the beating. The crowd of Irish vigilantes then were blown away by lasers shot by the blue aliens.

A drunken, homeless man named Otis Hanlon was passed out on the sidewalk when the noise from the invasion woke him. Otis was 55 years old. Otis woke up with a pounding headache. He was disgruntled about the way his life had turned out. He blamed society for his downfall, instead of taking responsibility for his laziness. Otis had spent most of his days and nights in the Dublin Woods, completely away from society. Otis Hanlon was a hermit. He was only at the fair to buy alcohol. He had drunk a lot of whiskey last night.

"Who the fuck woke me up?" shouted Hanlon. Then he chucked a whiskey bottle at one of the aliens. The whiskey bottle shattered instantly when it hit the alien in the chest, but the alien was unharmed because of the battle suit it wore. The alien turned around and saw an enraged bum off the street shaking his fist in anger in its direction. The alien fired a laser right at Hanlon's chest.

Hanlon groaned in pain. The laser melted his chest and burned his internal organs. Otis Hanlon died at 9:11 a.m. on Halloween morning.

The Egyptians and the four blue aliens just kept slaughtering people. The mummy shot flaming arrows at the fairgoers who were attempting to flee the fair. It was a complete bloodbath at the Dublin Halloween Fair.

***

David Patrician had just taken four shots of rum at his house a little while ago and was now heading toward the Dublin Halloween Fair. Along his travels, he noticed the Halloween Fair being attacked by hostiles from some distance away. David became a little nervous when he saw a war occurring before his eyes. David had a small fishing knife in his pocket, but he felt he needed more protection. David ran away from the invasion and began thinking of counterattack war strategies against these terrorists.

***

The Egyptians and the four blue aliens hovered around the mummy and safeguarded its evil heart as they moved along Irish territory, recklessly firing their ammunition at the Irish. The Egyptians soon marched on and prepared to swarm the battlement.

***

A woman named Paula McFrancis was at the Halloween Fair with her best friend Hayley McBrier. Paula and Hayley were childhood friends who had known each other for 38 years, ever since they were five years old. They were neighbors who had grown up together in Dublin. Paula and Hayley had been enjoying themselves at a small jewelry hut at the fair when it suddenly got raided. They both noticed chaos in the distance, and they could hear screaming as a crowd of Irish people at the fair ran for their lives. Paula and Hayley fled the area as quickly as they could. They were running side-by-side, five feet away from each other. Four blue aliens shot lasers toward them as they ran for their lives. Paula looked to her left and witnessed her best friend get blown away by a laser and killed. The laser struck Hayley in the back of her neck and blew her head off.

"No! Hayley!" shouted Paula. Paula ran away from her enemies as quickly as she could and never looked back. The four blue aliens were a few hundred feet away from her. They missed her with every shot and never bothered to chase after her.

Paula arrived home at 9:24 a.m. She was hysterical. Her husband and her son came to her aid immediately. Her husband, William, and her 17-year-old son, Clayton, became very nervous.

"Honey, what's the matter?" asked William.

"The Dublin Halloween Fair just got ambushed by a bunch of fuckin' terrorists!" shouted Paula.

"Jesus! Are you alright?" asked William.

"I made it out of there safely, but Hayley was killed. Her fuckin' head got blown off," said Paula.

"Hayley was killed? Jesus, that's terrible. I'm so sorry, Paula. Just try your best to relax and control your breathing. I think you're in shock."

Paula began to shiver uncontrollably. William stood by her side and did everything he could at that moment to comfort his traumatized wife. Ten seconds later, Paula's shivering came to an end.

"Mom, are you going to be alright?" asked Clayton in a very worried tone of voice.

"This was terrible to witness, but I have to be grateful I made it out of there safely," said Paula.

"Is there anything we can do to help you get through this terrible ordeal, honey?" asked William.

"As a matter of fact, there is. I need both of you to go to the battlement right now and help our fellow soldiers out in a time of war," said Paula.

"What are you fuckin' nuts, honey? We're not cut out for that kind of shit," said William. Paula gave them both a dirty look. She was extremely stressed out from the invasion. Suddenly, she looked at her husband and her son and saw how mentally and physically weak they really were. Then she stormed into the kitchen and grabbed two knives. She ran back toward them and said to them, "It's time for both of you fuckin' pussies to man up! Take these knives and go to the damn battlement right now before I stab both of you to death!"

Paula had the knives pointed at them both. She had a knife in her left hand and a knife in her right hand, and the blades were pointed a few inches away from their stomachs. The cursed clover implanted in the mummy's black heart was slowly beginning to poison her mind with evil thoughts. Paula had a crazy look in her eyes. William and Clayton were very nervous.

"Mom, what the hell has gotten into you?" said Clayton. "Please just calm down."

Paula continued to look at her husband and her son with a hostile glare. William and Clayton nervously stood there silent for a few seconds, worrying about their safety.

"Just shut up and do what your mother says, Clayton," said William, very worried. The two cowardly men each grabbed a knife and left the house. They had no weapons training and were both nervous as hell. William and Clayton headed to the battlements.

CHAPTER 12

Butch McPherson was close to his home. He was going there to grab the deed to his dwelling. Before he arrived, he noticed that David Patrician was already standing there in front of his doorstep, waiting. It was 9:33 a.m. David had only been waiting there for a minute.

"Butch, Ireland is under attack! Egyptian terrorists have waged war on us, and the Halloween Fair has just been invaded. Just as I was heading to the fair, I noticed the invasion in the distance. I got the fuck out of there quick because all I've got on me for protection right now is a measly fuckin' fishing knife in my pocket. I'll need more weapons, and so will you and the rest of the crew. We've got to come up with a good idea for a counterattack because Egyptian soldiers are after our land."

"What? They're after my lucky, four-leaf clover!"

"This is no time to be fuckin' around and playing games right now, McPherson! We're at war as we speak. We need to help in any way we can. We're trained soldiers."

David took a close look at McPherson's face. Then he looked at his neck and saw scratches and bruises. David gave his friend a strange look and said, "Jesus, man, what the fuck happened to you last night? Did you get into a fight or something? You look like hell."

"Oh, um, I went to the Dublin Brewery last night, and when I left, these three fuckin' idiots picked a fight with me. I took a little bit of a beating from them, but I managed to fight back and eventually, they all fled."

"They sound like a bunch of goddamn cowards," said David. "But remember I wanted to fuckin' strangle you last night when you fucked me over on the money you promised me upon completion of the cave project. Apparently, we've got much bigger problems on our hands with this goddamn invasion. Dublin is under attack as we speak."

"David, you need to calm down, and you need to listen to me very carefully. We're under attack because of this four-leaf clover, whether you want to believe it or not. Our best move right now is to gather up Kilgore, Garrison, and Ferguson, and we all need to retreat to the cave. Our soldiers will take out most of the invaders. Our last line of defense will be in the cave we built. This is why I fucked you over on the $5,000—I didn't have a choice. I knew someday we'd be invaded; I just didn't think it would be so soon. I'm just grateful the cave project was completed last night because it's the key to our victory. Now let's quit fuckin' around and grab the rest of the crew."

"You better be right, McPherson."

"Once you start to believe in the magical power of this four-leaf clover, you'll realize I'm right."

"For the last time, McPherson, shut the fuck up about that stupid clover!"

The two men hurried down the back hills of the Dublin Mountains. Soon after, they arrived at Kilgore's house. They knocked on Kilgore's door. Kilgore answered.

"We're under attack," said David. "Grab your belongings quickly, and let's get the fuck out of here. We need to get Garrison and Ferguson and let them know what's going on. We're all heading to the cave. Let's go."

"Jesus Christ! I was sleeping. I just got up a few minutes ago. Thanks for coming by. I'll be quick." Before Kilgore was about to gather up a few of his belongings, he looked at McPherson's face and noticed the swollen nose, scratches, and bruises on his neck. "Your face and your neck look swelled up. Are you alright, McPherson?"

"Yes, I'm fine," replied McPherson. "I got into it with these three drunk assholes last night at the Dublin Brewery. I held my own, and they won't be fucking with me again."

"OK, man," said Kilgore. "I'm just glad to hear that you're alright, buddy."

"Yeah, Yeah. Now quit stalling and let's get the fuck out of here," replied McPherson. Kilgore grabbed his keys, a candlelit lamp, a bow and arrow, and a sword. He locked the door to his small house.

They headed to Garrison's house, and a minute later, they arrived. Garrison heard loud noises in the distance—the chaos from the invasion. Garrison had just gotten up ten minutes earlier; the loud noises had woken him up. He'd spent the last five minutes with an ax in his hand, peeking out the window of his house. He was protecting his house from intruders.

Garrison saw Kilgore, Patrician, and McPherson all running toward his dwelling. He unlocked the door and let his friends in.

"What the fuck is going on out there? Are we being invaded?" said Garrison.

"Yes, we are," replied David.

Garrison looked at McPherson and noticed the swelling on his nose and the scratches and bruises on his neck. "You look like hell. Did someone attack you, McPherson?"

"I had a scuffle outside of the Dublin Brewery last night, and I don't feel like discussing it right now," said McPherson.

"OK, I understand. Sorry I asked," said Garrison.

"Don't worry about it. I'm fine! But we really do need to get the fuck out of here right now," said McPherson.

"We're heading to the cave, right?" said Garrison.

"Yes. But we got to grab Ferguson first," said McPherson.

"I'm ready," said Garrison.

Garrison left his house with an ax in his hands. He locked the door to his small house. The four men ran half a mile up the hill to Ferguson's house and pounded on the door. Ferguson didn't answer. He was passed out drunk on the couch in his living room.

"Ferguson, wake the fuck up! Dublin is under attack. We've got to leave," yelled McPherson through the window.

There was no answer. McPherson grew impatient.

"Hey, Garrison, let me see that fuckin' ax," said McPherson. Garrison handed it to him, and McPherson grabbed it forcefully and took it. McPherson swung the ax at Ferguson's door a few times. The door weakened, and McPherson kicked it open. McPherson gave the ax back to Garrison and then entered the house. The noise caused Ferguson to wake up.

"Come on, Ferguson!" said McPherson. "We got to get the hell out of here now. We're at war. Dublin is under attack. We need to head to the cave. Hurry up and let's go!"

"What the fuck, man! You busted my goddamn door! You owe me a new one, you fuckin' asshole!"

"I'm sorry about your door. Didn't you hear a word I said? We're under attack. We need to head to the cave. Come on, move!" yelled McPherson. He forcefully grabbed Ferguson's arm. Ferguson just resisted McPherson and stayed on his couch.

"I'm not going anywhere until I get my goddamn pay for this week," said Ferguson in a disgruntled tone.

"You'll get it later, Ferguson. Now quit stalling and get the fuck off the couch right now, and let's get moving! We need to head to the cave!"

"All right, all right, already. I'm fuckin' hungover. Just give me a damn minute to get up, for Christ's sake," said Ferguson.

Ferguson looked at McPherson's face. He saw that McPherson had a busted-up nose and scratches and bruises on his neck. He looked at McPherson oddly for a second.

"Dude, what the hell happened to your face? You look like shit, man," said Ferguson. McPherson became aggravated with Ferguson. He came up with the best lie he could at the moment.

"I was wrestling with your mother last night, and the bitch likes to play rough."

Ferguson laughed softly and said, "Come on, man. Don't talk about my fuckin' mother that way. What really happened to your face?"

"It's none of your fuckin' business, Ferguson. Now get the fuck off the couch right now and let's get moving you drunk bastard," said McPherson. Soon after, Ferguson got up as McPherson helped pull him off the couch.

"I can't believe you broke my fuckin' door, man!" said Ferguson.

"I'll fix it for you some other time. Forget about the goddamn door, Ferguson," said McPherson. Together they exited Ferguson's house.

"All right, we are all here. Time's wasting. Let's head to the cave," said McPherson. They all hurried up the hill and headed to the cave.

CHAPTER 13

The Egyptians marched forward on the Irish terrain and headed toward the battlements. They were hiding around the corner of a waterfall. The Egyptian army had just arrived there a few minutes earlier, now down to 924 soldiers. The Irish had fought back and killed 76 Egyptian soldiers. Nearly 500 Irish people had died in the attacks. The Irish were losing the war. The Egyptian army was waiting to storm the battlements on the mummy's command.

"Show no mercy and kill our enemy!" shouted the mummy. The Egyptian soldiers marched forward toward the battlement. The four blue aliens were safeguarding the mummy, who was experiencing heart problems. McPherson's clover was causing the mummy minor pain.

The mummy rounded the corner of the waterfall, with its army surrounding it. Irish soldiers were prepared. Many Irish soldiers and brave Irish folks stood by the battlements to defend their land. There were many men and women, both young and old. There were 1,268 Irish people prepared to fight back against the vicious Egyptian army. Flaming arrows were shot from both sides of battle. A few flaming arrows bounced off the four blue aliens. The four blue aliens started shooting lasers at the Irish, many of whom died. Egyptian soldiers were also getting slashed with swords and falling. Both sides of the battle were now suffering many casualties.

Connor McArthur was in one of the defense towers. He looked down at the massacre below him. He had a flaming arrow arched and a clear shot at the mummy's chest.

"I've got a clear shot at a hostile," shouted McArthur. He released the flaming arrow, and it struck the mummy in the middle of its chest.

The mummy yelled in pain. "Oh, fuck! My heart!" it exclaimed, then collapsed to the ground. The mummy was stunned. It was on fire. The four blue aliens had to smother the fire quickly. They did so. One of the aliens pulled the flaming arrow out of the mummy's chest. There was black blood oozing from the arrow and the mummy's heart. The aliens applied an ointment to stop blood loss. Then, two of the aliens started using mini surgical lasers on the mummy's chest, sealing up the skin around the mummy's heart.

The other two aliens began shooting their laser guns at the defense tower. They were shooting at Connor McArthur's fortress. The stone pillars were crumbling all around him. Men to the left and right of him were dying. William and Clayton had just arrived at the battlement. They ran up the spiral staircase, holding their knife blades down by the sides of their right hips as they ran up the stairwell. They were afraid they were going to stab someone who was on their side by accident, so they carried their knives this way for safety purposes.

"Daddy, I'm really scared," said Clayton.

"Me too, son," replied William.

They both continued to head up the stairwell, despite their nerves. A few seconds after they reached the top of the stairwell, William was shot with a laser in the chest and died instantly. He died at 10:18 a.m. William McFrancis was 46 years old.

"No! Daddy!" yelled out Clayton as he witnessed the horror. He stood there frozen in fear for a split second. More stones were falling on this defense tower. There were stone pillar barriers constructed above these defense towers. These stone barriers were being struck by multiple laser shots and crumbling down on many of these Irish soldiers, killing them instantly. Connor McArthur was five feet away from Clayton.

"What the fuck are you doing, kid?" shouted Connor as he grabbed Clayton McFrancis and dove out of harm's way. Clayton had dropped his knife on the ground nearby him, then quickly picked it up. He pointed the blade of the knife downward by his right hip and held it carefully. Connor picked up Clayton and ran away from these falling stones. He ran to the front end of the defense tower. There was a stone wall built all around the outside perimeter of this defense tower. The stone wall was three feet high. He put Clayton down next to the stone wall.

"Take cover, kid!" shouted McArthur. They both ducked down.

Clayton whimpered.

"Jesus, kid! What the fuck is the matter?"

"My daddy just got killed," said Clayton, as tears poured from his eyes.

"I'm sorry about your father, kid, but we're at war right now, and you're fucking things up," shouted Connor at the cowardly young Irishman. Connor noticed the knife in Clayton's hand. Clayton continued to whimper.

"You don't know what the fuck you're doing, kid! Let me see this goddamn fuckin' thing!" shouted Connor. He quickly grabbed the knife away from Clayton. Connor peeked over the stone wall of the defense tower very slowly and carefully. He looked down at the two aliens. Connor ducked down quickly.

The two aliens never saw Connor McArthur. The two aliens were shooting lasers at the defense tower, and they were not looking in Connor's direction at that particular moment. Connor stood up quickly. He chucked the knife downward. Then he immediately took cover.

The two aliens shooting lasers at the defense tower didn't see Connor stand up and chuck the knife. Connor knew how to remain covert in battle. Connor noticed these two hostile aliens were aiming their lasers at a section of the defense tower forty feet from where he and Clayton were hiding. He knew the two aliens never saw where he was hiding. The knife spun rapidly down from the tower and hit one of the aliens directly in the chest.

The tip of the knife dented instantly as it ricocheted off the alien's battle suit. The alien was furious. It shot lasers at the top of this defense tower. So did the other blue alien. Clayton leaned upward very slowly and peeked down at the ground below the defense tower. When he did so, the two aliens saw a small skull bop upward just a little bit. They fired their laser guns at their enemy.

Connor noticed Clayton peeking upward, and made another attempt to save his life.

"Jesus, kid! Take cover, for Christ's sake!" shouted Connor. When Connor pulled Clayton back down, the aliens shot their lasers at the stone pillars where these two men were hiding. Clayton was hit with a laser, and part of his skull melted. Stones then came crashing down on him. Clayton McFrancis died instantly. The lasers and debris went soaring right by Connor McArthur.

Connor managed to stay low as he tucked and rolled five feet to his left side and saved himself from the laser shots and crushing debris. He never dropped his bow and arrow during all this chaos, as he held onto his only weapon tightly. Connor headed toward the spiral staircase of the fortress. He ran down part of the stairwell on the defense tower. He crouched down and remained silent. Connor had an arrow aimed down the stairwell as he waited to defend himself against his attackers.

The aliens managed to heal the mummy's black heart. The surgery took a little less than five minutes.

The mummy awakened. "My heart is losing power. I can feel that the other clover is nearby." It looked up at the battlement. Then it slowly rolled its body around and looked at the waterfall near the Dublin River.

The mummy shouted, "The Irish are protecting something valuable in this cave! That's why the battlement is located here. The other clover is in the cave!"

A few Egyptian soldiers shielding the mummy in battle had heard the mummy speak. The mummy pointed over to the cave and then pointed to its evil heart. The four blue aliens knew where to strike next, as did many of the Egyptian soldiers. The mysterious cave was about to be raided.

CHAPTER 14

The green aliens had been searching the universe for forty-four years for the blue aliens responsible for their clover theft. They had two spacecraft searching the universe. These two spaceships flew across the universe and had been in communication the entire time. Their computer technology was linked to both ships.

The aliens aboard both spaceships were also down to their last morsels of food and water. One spacecraft was five miles outside of Earth's orbit, and the other spacecraft was about eight miles outside of Earth's orbit. The two spacecraft had just picked up a signal coming from a planet nearby, with signs of intelligent life.

Something strange suddenly happened. The green aliens began to receive a heavy reading from a specific location on Earth. That location was the cave in Dublin, Ireland. Both ships followed this signal. The green aliens were curious as to what they would discover.

CHAPTER 15

The four blue aliens and the mummy marched forward toward the cave. The blue aliens were circling the mummy as they walked forward. The aliens opened fire on the Irish soldiers trying to stop them. Many Irishmen were taken out. More Egyptians were also dropping dead by the second. Nearly half of the Egyptian soldiers were badly wounded or dead, but they still had 522 soldiers left. The Irish were putting up a much better fight now that the war was occurring near the battlement.

When the mummy and the four blue aliens were 100 feet from the cave entrance, two alien spaceships hovered 2,000 feet above the cave. Their radio beacons were still picking up the bizarre readings. The green aliens looked down at the battle that was occurring below between the Irish and the Egyptians. They were beginning to believe that this strange signal from the radio beacon was coming from their missing clover. From the sky, they could also see their enemies. These green aliens could all see the four blue aliens hovering around a mysterious mummy. They knew who to fire upon.

 The green aliens began shooting lasers down at the blue aliens. They aimed at the mummy and hit it a few times. The mummy was struck in the back with a few laser shots but only received slight burns. The blue aliens and the mummy looked up at the sky. The blue aliens knew the spacecraft belonged to their rival species. The blue aliens returned fire at the two alien spacecrafts, which took minimal damage from the lasers at such a distance.

The mummy was hit with another laser in the back. It roared in anger.

Then it did something it had never done before. The mummy pointed its arm up toward the two spacecrafts high in the sky and roared in anger again, this time even louder than before.

A second later, a heavy wind gust came, followed by a giant tornado. The mummy groaned, grabbed its heart, and collapsed to the ground. The aliens came to the mummy's aid immediately and began doing a surgical procedure on the mummy's heart.

As the mummy collapsed, Butch McPherson was barricaded at the end of the cave. His entire crew managed to retreat to a secret back entrance of this cave, completely unseen by the Egyptian soldiers. They were waiting in defense. They could hear the war going on around them from within this dark, enclosed cave. McPherson's clover was in a satchel in his right pocket. The clover burned McPherson in his upper right leg, which was odd because it had never done anything to harm him before. McPherson yelled in pain, then looked at the burn on his upper right leg.

"What the hell caused my lucky clover to do something awful like this to me?" he wondered. He debated for a second whether the clover was becoming cursed. He tried to get the clover burn and this curse off his mind, but it puzzled him while he waited for intruders at the end of this dark cave. He remembered what his friend David had said about this clover producing bad karma. It was messing with his mind a little bit. He tried to stay focused on battle instead.

***

The green aliens dropped a bomb on the mummy. Their plan was to blow it up before it entered the cave. The bomb had a 15-second timer on it before detonation, but the bomb got caught up in the giant tornado. The bomb was redirected in a path toward both of the spacecrafts. It exploded in the tornado and sent both ships on a crash course, landing 2,000 feet below.

The green aliens began panicking. One of the spaceships crashed right into one of the defense towers. Connor McArthur was still on this tower, crouching down near the stairwell. He never saw the ship come crashing down on his fortress. He and twenty of his soldiers died instantly when the ship crashed.

Soon after, a massive tidal wave from the Dublin River washed away the other defense tower and the battlement. The tidal wave was 300 feet high. Two green aliens died instantly from the crash into the defense tower. The other spacecraft crashed into the Dublin River, and the tidal wave then forcibly took control of the spaceship.

When the tidal wave settled, the spaceship sank in the river. The blue aliens were shooting lasers at it as it crashed down into the river. One of the green aliens died in this spacecraft, and one was still alive.

CHAPTER 16

It was 3:13 p.m. About four hours had passed since the tidal wave came crashing down on the city of Dublin. The tidal wave had flooded part of the city and it had taken almost four hours for most of the flooding to settle down. Massive flooding still existed in a three-mile stretch of damage. The Dublin River had become very shallow after this tidal wave. There was wreckage everywhere. The battlement was destroyed. So were the two defense towers. Crushed stone chunks littered the ground. Dead bodies floated everywhere.

The surviving green alien was very disoriented from the crash. The green alien had taken quite a beating as it had pulled muscles in its neck and shoulders and had a mild concussion. The battle suit that the green alien wore was the only reason it was able to survive the crash into the Dublin River. The battlesuit was stolen from the blue alien race on their home planet 143 years ago. The green alien was fifteen feet deep in the river, stuck in the spaceship for close to four hours. Part of the spacecraft was a few feet above water. The green alien took a flame torch and a mini laser to the metal wall inside of the spaceship and managed to weld through it to create an exit.

The green alien swam upward from the shallow river. When it managed to swim to the surface, it swam behind a giant rock located in the river and hid from the battle. The green alien just waited and hid for a few moments, spying on the mummy and the four blue aliens.

The four blue aliens noticed that the mummy had come to again. The cursed mummy had created a massive magnetic storm from the power of the four-leaf clover implanted in its evil black heart. It was a new power it had developed. The war was making it angry; it wasn't used to other lands fighting back as hard as the Irish had managed to fight back.

The negative energy from the clover implanted in the mummy's heart was what caused McPherson to be burned by his four-leaf clover. This happened as a result of positive and negative energy accumulating in both of these magical clovers. The horrific battle was what was causing the energy from the clovers to merge from different locations. This had never happened before because these two four-leaf clovers had never been this close to each other.

The mummy got up slowly. It and the aliens looked around the terrain for any survivors. There appeared to be none. The magnetic storm created by the mummy had killed all the soldiers in sight. However, creating this storm had taken a lot of energy out of the cursed mummy. The hunt for the other four-leaf clover was keeping the mummy determined to march forward, despite feeling battle fatigued. Hundreds of Irish and Egyptian soldiers lay dead on the ground.

The mummy and the four blue aliens moved ahead. They walked toward a crevasse between a rock. It was an entrance to the cave. When they entered, the green alien was a few hundred feet away, hiding behind a rock in part of the Dublin River that had become shallow due to the tidal wave. Water from the Dublin River was slowly draining from steep hills and back into the river. Some of the town of Dublin below the hills had gotten hit by this massive tidal wave, which had crushed many dwellings and instantly killed most of the innocent people inside of them.

When the tidal wave had settled down, a few homes had only minimal flooding, and the residents had sustained only minor injuries. The tidal wave had damaged a three-mile stretch of the city. The water from the tidal wave in the Dublin River was flowing through some of the lower passageways and tunnels in the cave.

The green alien watched the mummy and the four blue aliens approach the entryway to the cave. The green alien revealed itself from behind the giant rock and began to shoot lasers above the cave, attempting to crush the mummy and the aliens with falling debris from the cave. The green alien took cover behind the giant rock. The mummy and the blue aliens realized they were being fired upon. When they all turned around, they couldn't see a shooter. They noticed more and more debris from above, falling on them.

One of the blue aliens returned fire near where the green alien had been hiding. A few of the blue aliens' laser shots hit the giant rock and crumbled a small part of it, and the rest of the laser shots hit nothing but air. The blue alien moved forward and began to forcefully push the others forward toward the cave entryway. Small pieces of debris kept falling on them. The green alien revealed itself from behind the giant rock and fired more lasers at the cave entryway. Then the green alien took cover behind the giant rock again. Larger pieces of dirt, rocks, and green vines were rapidly falling on the mummy and the four blue aliens. All of them moved quickly. Three of the aliens made it inside the cave, and the mummy also made it inside the cave.

The one blue alien who returned laser fire toward an unseen enemy's direction was crushed by a large piece of debris, as many other pieces crumbled around it. The mummy and the three other aliens looked behind them and saw the blue alien's hands wiggling around under the debris. More of the cave entryway began to crumble. The mummy and the three blue aliens couldn't see the alien's body trapped underneath the debris anymore, but they could hear it suffering and squealing. Too much of the cave had crumbled. There was nothing the mummy or the three blue aliens could do to save the other blue alien. It would die within a week from starvation and dehydration. The three blue aliens and the mummy were frustrated over this casualty. The remaining three blue aliens safeguarded the mummy as they slowly headed down a tunnel in the cave.

CHAPTER 17

The three blue aliens and the mummy continued moving forward in the dark, mysterious cave. They entered a room. It was the emergency supply room. The three aliens and the mummy were beginning to think the supply room they'd discovered was built for war purposes, and they began to fear what was ahead.

The layout of the cave was unknown to them. They'd already witnessed a casualty from the falling debris crushing the blue alien. The blue aliens weren't used to this. The mummy wasn't expecting this, either. They knew their safety was now jeopardized after entering this cave. They weren't even sure how to exit the cave, now that the debris had crushed and blocked the entryway. The mummy and the three blue aliens were still determined to move forward and discover more of this cave. The mummy could sense the other clover nearby and knew it was coming closer and closer to fulfilling its evil destiny.

The mummy and the aliens didn't even bother grabbing the weapons in the supply room. The weaponry wasn't as advanced as the technology of their laser guns. The three blue aliens safeguarded the mummy as they exited the emergency supply room and slowly moved down a tunnel.

Kilgore was waiting near one of the traps. He could hear movement in the distance. He put down his sword and grabbed a bow and arrow. The three blue aliens and the mummy moved forward, and Kilgore thought about shooting his arrow at first, but he decided to wait and let the traps get one of the intruders first. There was a pile of large rocks stacked on top of each other on a part of the tunnel in this cave. McPherson had piled these rocks in that location on purpose. They were meant to collapse if stepped on. The rocks covered a ten-foot-long distance in the middle of a path in the cave. This tunnel was on higher ground in the cave. The rocks were meant to appear and feel stable enough to hold some weight. However, there were weak spots in the middle of these rocks, and the pile was meant to collapse in the middle.

There was a way past it. McPherson and his crew navigated around this area by hugging part of the wall of the tunnel on the left side. They could slowly and safely tiptoe around this area, avoiding disaster. Below these rocks was a 100-foot drop into a disgusting hole piled twenty feet high and filled with feces and urine from human beings and animals. There were maggots, slugs, and flies swarming the fecal matter McPherson had been dumping into this pit for ten years, creating a trap for hostiles.

Kilgore hid around the corner of the cave as the aliens and the mummy moved forward. They noticed the rocks along the path. They stopped moving for a moment. One of the aliens tested the durability of the rocks. They seemed durable enough to walk along, but something about it still seemed a little risky to them. The blue alien, who tested the rocks for durability, pointed to itself, then toward the distance ahead of them. They knew to move over these rocks one at a time.

The blue alien who felt the rocks' durability began slowly and cautiously tiptoed forward, using a small light it had connected to its battle suit. It took five slow steps, and no rocks shook. The alien still hesitated for a moment, then moved forward again very slowly.

After a few more cautious steps, one of the rocks wiggled just a little bit, slightly jolting the blue alien off-balance. The wiggle stopped. The blue alien was nervous about moving forward. It took another slow step, and the rocks remained stable. As soon as the blue alien took another slow step, the rocks collapsed. The blue alien began to panic and squeal. The rocks and the blue alien fell 100 feet below into the well filled with horrendous urine and feces. The alien began to move its arms and legs in panic and continued to squeal. The rocks were falling all around the trapped blue alien. Some of the rocks sank, and others just remained in the middle and atop this nasty scum pile.

The alien had a protective breathing mask on, but with the magnitude of human and animal waste all around it, the mask did no good. The blue alien could smell the disgusting odor from the pile it had been trapped in. The alien began to vomit inside its breathing mask and started choking on its own vomit. The blue alien died of suffocation about a minute after it tumbled into the nasty well. The two blue aliens and the mummy watched from above in horror.

Kilgore lit a flame on the tip of his arrow, then revealed himself from his hiding spot nearby. He shot a flaming arrow at one of the blue aliens. The arrow did no harm to the alien's body because of the battle suit it was wearing. Both remaining blue aliens returned fire at Kilgore. Their lasers hit Kilgore directly in the chest. Kilgore groaned in pain, then fell to the ground and died. The lasers melted the flesh and organs in part of his chest. Dutch Kilgore was 45 years old. The two blue aliens and the mummy turned around and began moving quickly away from the rocks. The two aliens used their mini-flashlights to see in the darkness ahead of them.

As they went on to search the other tunnels of the cave, the mummy began to feel a strain in its heart. The mummy became dizzy and collapsed; the stress from the clover war had caused its heart to fail. The two blue aliens came to the mummy's aid immediately. They performed quick tests and began pumping little electrical devices into the mummy's heart.

Five minutes later, the mummy opened its eyes and twitched a little. It was awake again.

CHAPTER 18

The green alien had been trying to enter the cave for the last twenty minutes. It had gotten stuck in some debris while crawling in. Specifically, the green alien's foot got caught on a heavy boulder. However, it was very close to making it through the debris. The alien was hungry, thirsty, and tired from trying to shake free. It got dizzy and rested for a minute in this dark cave.

Somewhere down below was the blue alien who had returned laser fire near the cave. The blue alien was crushed by dirt and rocks and slowly suffering to death. A giant rock once blocking part of the cave exit had just rolled down to the ground. Other smaller pieces of rocks, dirt, and vines also fell to the ground.

The green alien was still stuck, but now it could see a dark passageway ahead. It desperately attempted to wiggle itself free, but it couldn't get out. The green alien was dehydrated. It just rested for a moment, hoping that someone would come to its rescue soon.

CHAPTER 19

The mummy and the two blue aliens were on the move. They were walking more and more cautiously with each step, being careful not to fall into one of the traps. They walked to a lower level of the cave. Part of this level stunk of urine and feces. They headed there despite the smell because they wanted to peek into the pit to see if the blue alien was all right from the fall into the stinky hole. They all peeked into the trap.

The mummy had a sense of smell just like humans, because of its heart. The aliens also had a sense of smell. They could all smell the disgusting odor of feces and urine from the rank pit. They all looked down into the pit, and two of the aliens flashed lights down below. They all saw the blue alien lying dead, floating upright in the nasty well of feces and urine. They all shook their heads in frustration.

The mummy gagged from smelling the pit and said, "That is the most disgusting fuckin' thing I've ever smelled in my whole goddamn life. Let's get the fuck away from here now."

The aliens expressed how they felt about the bad smell by waving their hands quickly in front of their noses and turning their heads slightly sideways in disgust. The two blue aliens and the mummy began walking away from the rank pit. The mummy keeled over in agony. The aliens thought the mummy was experiencing heart failure again and knelt by its side, ready to help it. The mummy held its lower stomach and leaned over and gagged. It vomited in disgust from the smell of the rank pit, then coughed a few times. It was dizzy. The mummy's heart wasn't at full strength; it had lost a little bit of its power. The mummy needed a minute to rest. Then it got up slowly.

"Oh man, that fuckin' stinks!" said the mummy. The mummy and the two blue aliens moved on to another path of the cave.

CHAPTER 20

The mummy and the two blue aliens moved on slowly. They found a passageway to a new tunnel that led to a lower-level area of the cave. Water from the tidal wave had dripped into this section of the cave and was slowly dripping into deeper sections of this cave. This particular section of the cave had been dug deep, deep underground. It was one of the reasons the project had taken ten years to complete.

Garrison was waiting in this area. He was on the opposite side of an eight-foot-long wooden plank. The terrain around the plank was designed a little narrower in this section of the tunnel. The plank wasn't safe. It was a rotting piece of unsteady wood. Under this plank was a wooden pit of sharp spikes twenty feet below. The safe way around it was to get a running start and jump over it, clearing the eight-foot gap to the other side of the tunnel. Garrison and his fellow companions who'd built this cave knew this. Garrison saw the mummy and the two blue aliens in the distance. He looked over at them. He was holding an ax in his hands. They were some distance away.

"Come and get me, fucker!" yelled Garrison. He stuck his tongue out and taunted the mummy and the two blue aliens. He ran around the corner and vanished quickly. The two blue aliens proceeded forward. The mummy was angered by this five-foot-tall, Irish man playing games while a war was taking place. It found strength from this anger and charged forward, chasing after this annoying Irishman.

The mummy roared loudly, "I'm going to get you, you Irish prick!" Then it ran onto the plank. It took a couple of steps onto the plank, and then the plank collapsed.

The mummy yelled, "Ah, fuck!" and then it fell twenty feet into a wooden spike trap below. The mummy got stuck in the wooden spikes. It lay there for a minute, grunting in pain. It attempted to roll around in the cage. Pieces of the mummy's cloth were torn from its struggles in the spike trap. It continued to slowly roll around, attempting to free itself from the sharp wooden spikes, but it couldn't.

The mummy's heart was becoming weak again, and the aliens couldn't revive it. The mummy became dizzy. Seconds later, it snapped out of it and got very angry from falling into this trap. It didn't need heart surgery to find strength. It had the black magic from the evil clover implanted in its heart. The blue aliens kept it rejuvenated this long, but its heart was beginning to learn how to rejuvenate itself now. The mummy began to smirk.

Then the mummy laughed. "Ha, ha, ha, ha, ha!" The laugh echoed above the wooden pit, sounding very evil and dark.

Garrison became very nervous. He had run into a dead end in the cave. He thought this trap would have eliminated the mummy when it fell into it.

He was wrong. The mummy was alive and angry. Suddenly, the mummy turned into a cloud of vapor. It maneuvered its way upward. The mummy looked out of a bloodshot, purple-colored eye to help guide its way. It floated up quickly. It had never been able to do this before. The black magic from the implanted four-leaf clover in its cursed black heart gave it this supernatural ability. The two blue aliens were impressed when they saw the mummy turn to vapor and float its way free from the trap. They were now becoming a little more confident they would soon find the other four-leaf clover.

The mummy floated toward the dead end, where Garrison was standing with the ax in hand. Garrison had nowhere to run and nowhere to hide. The mummy floated in a vapor cloud right toward Garrison. Soon it was fifteen feet away from him. Garrison ground his teeth as he looked at the cloud of vapor that was the evil mummy. He looked at the hideous bloodshot purple eye. It freaked him out.

The mummy laughed again. "Ha, ha, ha!"

Garrison stood there frozen in fear.

"Come and get me, fucker," said the mummy in an evil voice. Then it floated toward Garrison aggressively.

Garrison swung his ax at the mummy, then loudly yelled out, "Ah!" The ax hit nothing but a foggy cloud of vapor, and it did no damage to the mummy, and the mummy then floated into Garrison's chest. It exploded. Garrison's body blew to pieces all over the dead-end section of the dark cave. Elton Garrison died in the dark cave at the age of 49. The mummy then formed itself back into a solid, immortal creature. It now had a new magical power.

CHAPTER 21

Ferguson was becoming very aggravated. He was still hungover and didn't want to go to war. He was crouching down near a trap where he'd been waiting for an hour. He could hear strange noises and yelling going on in other sections of the cave. He knew that some of his men were in trouble. He also had a feeling that some of these invaders had fallen into the traps. He knew his enemies were on the move somewhere in the cave.

The trap Ferguson was positioned near was in a higher section of one of the tunnels. It was a passageway leading to the end of a tunnel. Along this passageway was an unstable section of ground. A large hole was dug out and piled up with sticks and rocks. On top of these sticks and rocks was dirt that had been cautiously patted down. The sticks and rocks underneath were not visible. It was designed like this to appear as a normal spot in the tunnel that was stable to walk across.

Underneath this trap was a 1,000-foot drop to a lower section of the cave. Jagged rocks were located down at the bottom of this trap. The trick to getting around this trap without falling below was to tiptoe around the right side of the dirt slowly. There wasn't a lot of room to balance oneself, and hanging onto the rock wall on the side of the tunnel while tiptoeing along was necessary to keep one's footwork.

On the other side of this trap, where Ferguson was in position, spear in hand, there were many more passageways that led to more vicious traps, dead ends, and the end of the cave. The mummy and the two blue aliens headed in Ferguson's direction. Ferguson heard the footsteps of the invaders. He remained quiet and crouched down behind a rock located in the tunnel ten feet away from the trap, waiting for the mummy and the two blue aliens to approach the trap.

When they did, Ferguson revealed himself from behind the rock and chucked the spear with his left hand. He aimed right for the mummy's chest. The spear went soaring through the air. The mummy became frightened by the soaring spear and crouched down a little, as it quickly covered its chest with its hands, attempting to protect its heart from the spear. One of the blue aliens dove in front of the mummy and took the spear on its body armor. The tip of the sharp metal spear instantly dented, then bounced off the blue alien's battle suit. The alien landed on the ground.

Ferguson shouted, "Fuck!" when he noticed the spear did no damage to the blue alien. Ferguson began yelling and screaming loudly. The mummy stopped crouching in protection and looked toward Ferguson. It moved its left arm forward, pointed toward its enemy, and yelled, "Waste him!" to the two blue aliens. The two blue aliens fired lasers at Ferguson. One of the aliens was standing upright as it fired shots, and the other alien was on the ground and leaning sideways: firing shots toward its enemy. Ferguson's eyes opened widely when eight laser shots whizzed right past him in both directions. The lasers zoomed through the air and brightened the dark cave for a couple of seconds. The lasers hit a rock wall some distance away and crumbled part of it. The cave became very dark again. Ferguson turned around and ran for his life.

CHAPTER 22

Ferguson kept running. As the blue alien got up from the ground, it, the mummy, and the other blue alien moved forward toward their enemy. One of the blue aliens was a few feet ahead of its war companions and it marched forward quickly in pursuit of Ferguson and, in so doing, stepped on the trap.

The ground collapsed underneath the alien. The blue alien squealed and fell. The other blue alien and the mummy were on the trap when it had collapsed underneath, but they'd each only taken one step forward, and so had managed to jump back to safe ground behind them, and spared themselves from the treacherous fall. They both dove to the ground as rocks crumbled down to deeper ground, right near them. As Ferguson ran, he quickly looked over his left shoulder when he heard a loud noise. He saw his enemies: forty feet behind him. When he heard the rocks crumble and looked behind, he saw one of the aliens tumbling down. And he saw the other alien and the mummy diving away from the crumbling rocks. They looked like dark moving shadows to him. Ferguson only saw a brief glimpse of them. He turned his head forward and kept running. The mummy and the blue alien looked in the direction of their enemy. The mummy moved its left arm forward as it lay on the ground and pointed toward Ferguson and yelled, "Fuckin' waste him!" to the blue alien as Ferguson ran. The alien was on the ground and leaning over sideways as it fired four laser shots at Ferguson and missed. Ferguson kept running and didn't look back. He ran quicker when he heard laser shots fired. He saw four blue lasers zoom right past him and brighten up the dark cave for a second. He heard a noise and saw lasers crumble the rock wall ten feet in front of him. The cave became completely dark again. Ferguson ducked a little bit as he kept running. He ran past a left corner in a narrow tunnel and vanished from his enemies' site. The mummy and the blue alien were very angry. They both stood up. The mummy turned into vapor and traveled over the trap. It was moving slowly, looking ahead through its purple eye. After the mummy made it over the trap, it reconstituted itself back to an immortal creature. The mummy was temporarily out of energy. It needed to rest for a moment.

***

The blue alien that had fallen was 1,000 feet below, lying uncomfortably on jagged rocks. The alien was a little shaken up from the fall, however, it was alive and unharmed. The battlesuit had protected it from the fall. But the blue alien was now trapped below in these jagged rocks, with no way out. It would remain down there in this dark pit forever. With no food or water, it would die in a week.

***

Ten seconds later, the mummy reenergized itself. The mummy had limited mobility when it turned to vapor. It could only turn to vapor for so long. The clover that McPherson carried in his satchel was limiting the mummy's energy. The blue alien tiptoed slowly across the right side of this trap, holding onto the rocks on the side of the tunnel. It was only halfway across.

The mummy became impatient. It wanted the alien to hurry up and cross over the gap of the tunnel quicker because it wanted to kill Ferguson. The mummy shouted at the blue alien, "Hurry the fuck up, will you! That Irish prick is getting away!"

The alien didn't understand what the mummy had said. However, it knew the mummy was irate and impatient when it aggressively waved its left hand and pointed toward where the enemy had run. The alien was crossing over the dangerous gap as best it could. The blue alien reached over for the mummy's arm, and the mummy helped the blue alien with the final steps across the trap, pulling the alien out of harm's way as it shouted, "Come on, you fuckin' idiot," to the alien. The blue alien and the evil mummy began chasing after Ferguson.

CHAPTER 23

Ferguson was still on the run. He knew he could run down some of the tunnels without being caught in a trap. He looked behind for the mummy and the blue alien but could not see either of them. It was dark. Ferguson didn't want his enemies to find him, so he'd ditched his candlelit lamp.

Ferguson kept going farther and farther into the dark tunnels. He had a pretty good idea of how to navigate around these areas without using anything to brighten the way.

The blue alien and the mummy were confused. They didn't know which tunnel to search first. They headed down some of the tunnels back and forth a few different times. They were lost.

Ferguson was running in a passageway below them. The mummy and the blue alien could hear the footsteps below, and they looked at each other. Then they both pointed downward simultaneously. They knew their enemy was below them, running for his life. The alien and the mummy quickly made their way down to the lower levels of the cave. Ferguson continued to run into the cave.

David Patrician was hiding around a corner behind a rock. When he heard footsteps coming from nearby, he drew out a bow and arrow and aimed an arrow toward the noise of the footsteps. He peeked around the corner to see who was running. He put down his bow and arrow when he saw it was Ferguson.

"Hey, Ferguson! It's me, David," he said.

"David, is that you?" replied Ferguson.

"Of course, it's me, you fuckin' dimwit!"

Ferguson was relieved to see one of his own men still alive.

"Jesus, am I glad to see you! I saw a mummy and two fuckin' aliens running around near one of the traps. One of the aliens fell down in the dirt pit a few minutes ago. I fucked the thing over by luring it in my direction. The mummy and another alien are on the hunt for me. I threw a spear at one of the aliens, but their weaponry repelled it. If you see one of these creatures running around here, just run away immediately. They are too fuckin' dangerous to fight with their sophisticated body armor."

"Aliens are running around in this cave?" exclaimed David.

"Yes," said Ferguson. "And a possessed mummy. Just be careful. I know it seems farfetched, but I saw these evil creatures with my own eyes."

"I believe you," David said. "I've been hearing fucked-up noises coming from all around in here tonight. I think we should split up."

Ferguson shook his head. "That's a terrible idea, David. We need to stick together and get to an exit. And what about the others?"

"Unfortunately, they're all on their own, and the fate of their survival is completely up to them," said David.

"You know what the worst thing about today is, David?"

"No. What's that, Ferguson?"

"I never got my fuckin' paycheck for this week."

"Jesus, Ferguson. Will you just forget about your goddamn money for right now?" said David in an agitated tone of voice. "I'll double your pay for the week if we both make it out of this fuckin' cave in one piece. Now just shut the fuck up and stay focused."

David and Ferguson stood quietly for a moment. They could hear the footsteps of their enemies in the distance. David picked up his bow and arrow and aimed an arrow in the direction of his enemies.

"David, I just told you that our fuckin' weapons are useless against them. Put the fuckin' thing away and hide. They're coming for us," said Ferguson. David quickly put away his bow and arrow. They both took cover and hid behind the rock in desperation.

"Fuck this," David said. "I'm out of here."

He got up and ran away.

"David! Where the fuck are you going?"

David didn't respond. He just ran. Soon after, Ferguson got up from his hiding spot and took off running too. They ran on different paths around the dark cave for a few minutes. Neither of them could see where they were going. They eventually collided, and both fell to the ground.

"Ah, fuck!" yelled David.

"Damn it!" yelled Ferguson.

They were both dazed from the collision. It took both men a few seconds to get up, and, even then, they both got up a little slowly.

"Sorry, David. Are you all right?" asked Ferguson.

"Will you watch where you're going, you clumsy fuck!" replied David.

Ferguson didn't reply. He just hung his head in shame. When David turned around, he saw the mummy and an alien in the distance.

"Look out, Ferguson!" yelled David. Ferguson turned around and got blasted in the chest with a laser by the blue alien. Ferguson screamed in agony, then fell to the ground. Raymond Ferguson died at the age of 28. David dove out of harm's way and rolled down a steep tunnel. He landed well below onto jagged rocks. The mummy and the blue alien were on the hunt for him, but David Patrician was unconscious.

CHAPTER 24

The blue alien and the mummy ran around all over the cave, on the hunt for David Patrician. The mummy was becoming tired and breathing heavily. The mummy and the alien had no idea where their enemy was. They were determined to find him and kill him.

They eventually found a different path instead. They hadn't been down this part of the cave before. They were hoping to find their enemy roaming somewhere down this new path so they could waste him. David was nowhere to be found. The mummy became dizzy. It had no energy, so it rested on the ground for a moment. The blue alien hurried to the mummy's side and began to pull out mini-electrical equipment to revive the mummy. The mummy shoved the alien's hand away from its heart when the blue alien attempted a heart procedure.

"Get the fuck off me!" yelled the mummy. The mummy knew it wasn't in need of another heart revival. It needed the other four-leaf clover. The mummy could feel the energy from this other clover wearing it down.

The mummy suddenly found strength. It felt something in its evil heart. It got up from the ground and quickly marched forward, and the blue alien followed. The mummy suddenly knew where to go to battle for the other magical clover.

CHAPTER 25

The mummy and the blue alien marched forward, the mummy going where its instincts told it. As they neared the end of the cave, they marched down a steep, winding tunnel. The blue alien was lighting the way ahead of them. Suddenly, the path ended. There was a circular stone battleground, with jagged rocks below it.

McPherson was standing on the battleground, holding a sword in his right hand and an alloy shield in his left. He constructed his shield out of very durable metal. The alloy shield weighed sixty pounds. He knew the intruders would come after his clover, and that he had to make one final stand. McPherson fearlessly stood on this stone battleground, gazing at the mummy and the blue alien. The alien shot a laser at McPherson. McPherson blocked the laser with his alloy shield.

The mummy quickly vaporized itself. It tried to float inside McPherson's body and kill him, but it couldn't float forward. The clover in McPherson's pocket prevented this from happening. The mummy formed back into an immortal creature and drew its sword.

The blue alien charged forward at McPherson. McPherson just waited and let the alien run at him. The alien ran toward the middle of the battleground, but the stones underneath suddenly gave way and collapsed. The alien fell below into a pit of venomous snakes—thousands of them. McPherson had been capturing snakes for thirty years. For the past year, he'd been putting the captured snakes into this pit. It was one of his traps. He carefully placed the stone pillars around the middle of this area without any cement. He knew it would collapse if stepped on, and he knew where to move safely on this battleground.

The blue alien was trapped. It squealed and squirmed around in the snake pit, desperate to free itself from this awful trap. The alien began shooting its laser gun everywhere, and the beams hit the rock wall on the sides of the cave. A few snakes were instantly burned and killed by the laser shots. The other snakes crawled all around this helpless blue alien. More and more snakes crawled all around it. All these snakes weighed the blue alien down, and it could barely wiggle around anymore. It was becoming tiring. The battle suit was the only thing keeping it alive and exerting so much energy had made the blue alien very thirsty. The blue alien lay there and suffered in the snake pit. It would eventually die within a week from starvation and dehydration. The blue alien species would soon be extinct.

The mummy yelled, "I want your fuckin' clover!"

"Come and get it, asshole!"

The mummy and McPherson began to battle with swords on the circular battleground. They kept thrusting swords toward one another at rapid speed. They dodged and blocked each others' thrusts. They were both focused on battle. The mummy took a swipe at McPherson's right hip with its sword. The sword cut McPherson's army pants, and the satchel that his clover was stashed in fell to the ground. McPherson didn't notice this.

More and fancier sword swipes and sword blocks were exchanged. The mummy and General Butch McPherson were both skilled swordsmen. Neither could finish their enemy. They shifted over and kept circling around each other, trying to kill each other. McPherson was using his shield to protect himself as well. He blocked a few of the mummy's sword attacks with his shield. He swung the shield at the mummy a few times and struck it aggressively, angering the mummy. The mummy kept trying to strike McPherson with its sword, but it couldn't. McPherson just kept sword-fighting with the mummy, refusing to die.

A little leprechaun had been watching this battle from within a small crevice of the cave. It saw the satchel fall out of McPherson's army pants. It quietly moved toward the satchel on the battleground and picked it up. The leprechaun opened up the satchel to see what was inside. It reached its little hand into the satchel and pulled out a shining four-leaf clover. It looked at it in awe. The leprechaun put the clover back in the satchel and kept it. It softly giggled, then quickly ran back into the crevice in the rock wall and vanished.

The mummy and General McPherson never saw the little leprechaun. Their eyes were on each other and focused on battle. The mummy took a fast sword swipe at McPherson's chest. McPherson blocked this attack with his sword and counterattacked, exposing the mummy's chest. McPherson struck the mummy's black heart with his sword, and the mummy groaned in pain.

"Ah, fuck! My heart!" yelled the mummy.

Black blood oozed from the mummy's chest. The sword had black blood on it. Some of this black blood began to ooze onto the stones of the battleground. Stunned, the mummy dropped to the ground, appearing lifeless. McPherson approached the mummy with his sword drawn and poked at it. The mummy was motionless.

McPherson was convinced he'd killed this evil creature. He checked for his satchel in the right pocket of his army pants and noticed the army pants were cut and the satchel wasn't in his pocket. He looked all over the battleground for the satchel containing his lucky four-leaf clover, but he couldn't find it.

"No! My clover!" McPherson yelled. "My lucky Irish four-leaf clover! I lost it. Where the fuck is it?"

McPherson searched all over for his missing clover, but couldn't find it anywhere. He knew he needed to get out of the cave soon. He knew he needed to bury this cursed mummy in the same place he'd found his lucky four-leaf clover when he was six years old. He knew that the Devil would come and try to take the mummy's evil soul to hell. He poked at the mummy with his sword again. The mummy was unresponsive.

McPherson left his sword and alloy shield on the battleground and dragged the mummy down one of the tunnels. He kept dragging it until he reached one of the cave's exits. He noticed the tunnel was flooded with water from the tidal wave. He couldn't escape the tunnel from here. He would have to head to the other exit. McPherson dragged the mummy through more tunnels and passageways and headed for the exit of the cave, near the waterfall.

CHAPTER 26

McPherson continued moving through tunnels in the dark cave. He was dragging the mummy along with him, determined to bury this evil creature. His arms were becoming tired, as the mummy was very difficult to drag through this cave. It was heavy and still motionless. All of a sudden, McPherson started feeling dehydrated. He became lightheaded. He stopped dragging the mummy for a moment and drew out a bow and arrow to prepare to defend himself.

From fifty feet away, he saw a scary-looking blue alien with no clothing on its body. It hissed at him. Without hesitation, McPherson shot the arrow directly into the frightening blue alien's chest. The blue alien squealed in agony and dropped to the ground; it appeared dead from a distance. McPherson stormed over to this blue creature with an arrow drawn to see if it was dead. McPherson moved closer and closer to the blue alien. When he was three feet from it, he looked down at it. Suddenly, he snapped back to reality and realized he'd shot David Patrician in the chest with an arrow.

CHAPTER 27

"No! David!" yelled McPherson.

McPherson had hallucinated and mistaken David Patrician for a hostile blue alien. The reason this happened was that McPherson didn't have his lucky four-leaf clover on hand, and he was carrying the mummy's cursed clover instead. The mummy's curse was what caused McPherson to hallucinate in the cave and accidentally kill his partner.

McPherson was devastated. He had screwed his best friend out of $5,000 and killed him with an arrow. He thought for a second that he was dead and actually in hell. He yelled out loudly in the dark cave, "Ah!" and kicked the rock wall a few times in anger.

He soon calmed down and slowed his breathing down. "David, I'm so sorry," he said as he looked at his dead partner on the ground. He put away his bow and arrow and moved forward, dragging the mummy along with him. He saw Kilgore and Ferguson, dead, along his travels. He didn't recognize Garrison, but he saw pieces of human flesh in one location. He saw the dead alien floating in his trap of feces and urine. He saw the wreckage the traps had caused in the crazy cave.

He continued moving toward the exit, through all sorts of passageways and tunnels. He had to take a longer exit because he couldn't get the mummy's heavy corpse past some of the deep gaps in the tunnels that the traps had left behind. He continued moving down the dark tunnels, dragging the mummy along with him.

When McPherson was right around the corner from the emergency supply room, he put the mummy down. He went into the emergency supply room and grabbed a metal shovel. McPherson walked out of the room and grabbed the mummy by the arm. As he was dragging the mummy around the corner of a dark tunnel, he could hear someone or something squealing in agony. He stopped dragging the mummy and put down his shovel. He drew out his bow and arrow. He continued forward with an arrow drawn. He saw an alien wearing a battle suit caught under a rock. He could not tell immediately that the alien was green. General McPherson was prepared to shoot this alien, unsure if he was hallucinating or not. He hesitated to fire the arrow because he remembered what had happened minutes earlier in the cave when he accidentally wasted his best friend with an arrow, mistaking him for an alien.

He walked closer to the alien and noticed the alien's skin color was green. The alien didn't appear hostile. McPherson realized this green creature was in trouble and needed to get free from the rock trap. McPherson put away his bow and arrow and climbed up the pile of rocks and debris. He pulled the rocks with all his might. The alien squealed a few more times, then it shook free after McPherson moved the rocks away from its body.

The alien got up. McPherson and the green alien looked at each other then they made their way down the pile of rocks and debris. The green alien showed McPherson a small drawing it had of a green four-leaf clover. McPherson looked at the green creature oddly for a moment.

"I'm sorry," said McPherson. "I don't have my lucky four-leaf clover anymore. I lost it when I was battling the mummy."

The green alien didn't understand what McPherson was saying. They were both looking for missing clovers. McPherson took the green alien around the corner of the passageway. He showed the green alien the mummy. The green alien looked at the mummy and remembered firing lasers from its spaceship at this mummy as it was entering the cave earlier in the day. It remembered the blue aliens trying to protect it. It also knew the blue alien race was responsible for the clover theft on their home planet forty-four years ago.

The green alien was finally coming closer and closer to finding the lucky four-leaf clover from its home galaxy. It pointed to the picture of its green four-leaf clover drawing, then looked at McPherson. Then the alien pointed at the mummy. The green alien suspected the four-leaf clover was surgically implanted somewhere in the mummy. The green alien began doing an autopsy on the mummy. It began by rubbing an ointment on the mummy's chest to decrease blood flow. Then it took a mini laser to the mummy's chest.

As soon as the mini laser pierced a small section of the mummy's black heart, the green alien received a massive electric shock and instantly died, killed by the magical four-leaf clover.

"No!" yelled McPherson, when he saw the green alien drop to the ground and die. This was the last green alien of its species. The green alien race was now extinct. McPherson shook the alien to check and see if it had any signs of life. The green alien was motionless. McPherson got very angry and went back to the cave exit.

He began climbing atop the rock pile that was blocking the exit. He crawled up twenty feet and began moving rocks around, trying to get free from the cave. Rocks, dirt, vines, and debris continued to fall as McPherson attempted to create an exit. McPherson wanted out of this hellish cave. It took him three minutes to move enough rocks around to create an escape passage from the cave.

He walked back down the pile of rocks and debris, grabbed the shovel and the evil mummy, and dragged it up the rock pile. He grunted heavily and kept pulling the mummy behind him.

McPherson wiggled his way out. He threw the metal shovel onto the ground, then tugged and tugged and pulled the mummy out of the cave. He pulled the mummy forcefully and let it drop to the ground.

McPherson carefully made his way down the steep rocks. Then he stood up and looked all around. His eyes saw nothing but pure horror. He saw the wreckage from the tidal wave. He saw the stone pillars from the battlement and the two defense towers crushed all over the ground. He saw dead bodies all over the Dublin River, floating next to the war wreckage, as well as dead bodies from both sides of battle all over the ground. He saw swords, arrows, and axes all over the ground. He was war fatigued.

He yelled out, "No!"

No one around was alive to hear him. He grabbed his shovel. Then he grabbed the mummy by its right arm and began to drag it up the hill. McPherson was determined to bury the mummy in a ditch behind a patch of grass that was just up the hill. This was the same spot where he'd found his lucky four-leaf clover when he was a six-year-old kid. He remembered when he'd killed the baker Curtis Haynesworth there on Halloween night, forty-four years ago. He remembered when the Devil came from beneath the ground and took Curtis Haynesworth's soul and dragged it to hell. McPherson was sure the Devil would also come to drag the mummy's soul to hell. He headed uphill to the burial ground to send the mummy's evil soul to hell forever.

CHAPTER 28

It was 4:20 p.m. on Halloween in Dublin, Ireland. The sky was beginning to turn slightly dark. It began pouring rain. McPherson's arms were becoming tired from dragging the heavy creature up the hill. He was almost at the top of the hill. Dead Irish soldiers and dead Egyptian soldiers lay everywhere. McPherson just wanted to get to the patch of green grass atop the hill where he'd found his lucky four-leaf clover. He wanted to put this clover war to an end. He wanted his lucky four-leaf clover back.

McPherson reached the top of the hill and stopped dragging the mummy. There was a ditch ten feet behind the bright green patch of grass he was standing on. There was an unmarked tombstone next to the ditch. McPherson put the tombstone there thirty years ago, on Halloween night. There were also some dirt patches all along the ditch. He whacked the mummy in the face with his shovel, then dragged the mummy into the ditch. The ditch was eight feet deep. McPherson began shoveling dirt on top of the mummy.

Suddenly, from within the ditch, the blood vessels in the mummy's heart began to rejuvenate. When General McPherson stabbed the mummy in its heart with a sword, he thought he killed it. The sharp sword only pierced a small section of the mummy's black heart. The sharp sword never hit the clover. The mummy had been stunned and only appeared dead. From all the medical procedures the blue aliens had performed on it, and the implanted clover in the mummy's black heart, which was capable of black magic, this mummy was still very much alive on this frightening Halloween night. It opened its eyes within the ditch to see McPherson shoveling dirt on it.

The mummy struck its fist in the air. A massive bolt of lightning came zapping down onto the metal tip of General McPherson's shovel, causing him to drop dead on the ground next to the ditch. The Devil came floating up from the ditch and tried to grab McPherson's soul. However, the Devil missed Butch McPherson's soul. The ghost of General Butch McPherson knew immediately to float upward, safely away from the Devil, because he recalled seeing what this demon had done to Curtis Haynesworth's soul in this exact location forty-four years ago. The Devil could only float upward a few feet, and it couldn't reach McPherson's soul. The Devil floated back under the ditch and deep underground, back to hell.

The mummy got a massive burst of energy. It floated upward. The mummy and the ghost of General Butch McPherson gazed at each other in war mode. They were five feet away from each other. The ghost of General Butch McPherson saw that the mummy had a shiny, glowing, four-leaf clover implanted in its black heart. The mummy hissed at its enemy. Then the mummy reached out quickly with its left hand and tried to claw at its enemy, but it missed.

By the luck of the Irish, the ghost of General Butch McPherson floated away safely from the vicious attack. McPherson's ghost now had new intelligence that the Egyptian mummy had a four-leaf clover, implanted in its black heart that was capable of evil.

www.ingramcontent.com/pod-product-compliance
Lightning Source LLC
Chambersburg PA
CBHW042305070726
47818CB00009B/221